Lie No More

Terry Keys

Lie No More © 2017 Terry Keys

Get a free novel from Terry here https://terrykeys.authorreach.com/lead/c904c0ea

Check out the book trailer for my new book Death Toll Rising!
https://www.youtube.com/watch?v=JXvMkcJViiM

Lie No More

When the stakes get high enough – there is a killer inside us all. . .

Mild mannered Candice Harstows day started like any other day. And then it quickly turned into a nightmarish hell that she couldn't escape. With time running out and no one she could trust she sets a plan in motion that would change everything – forever.

Our lives are always one decision away from being irrevocably changed forever.
– Author unknown

Prologue

I want to start off by telling you about the second-worst day of my life. You're probably wondering why I don't skip this and just tell you about the worst day of my life, right? Well, just consider this foreplay.

The second-worst day of my life led to horrors that I never imagined were possible. Which is why I should start here.

It started out like any other day. My husband of twenty years, John, was already off to work. His law firm was busier than it'd ever been, and John was taking on more cases than he'd ever had to—which, among other things, had helped drive the wedge between us even deeper. Most nights now John worked late—really late. I'd come to expect it and had stopped waiting up for him many months ago. My friend Diane told me I was crazy for staying with him and that he had to have another woman. Said I needed to get one of those private investigators to check him out. John had been many things, and he wasn't a saint, but I knew he wasn't a cheater either. John was quite the flirt and had always been the life of the party, but I never doubted whether or not he was faithful to me. He loved me, and, most importantly, he adored our son, Max. Most couples who were married as long as John and me eventually drifted apart. If not all the way, at least a little bit. It's just what happens. I still loved him, and he still loved me, and that was all that mattered. While I thought about it, I sent him a text that said, I love you.

It was seven a.m., and I sat at the kitchen table drinking a cup of coffee, just like I did every day. Coffee in the morning, wine at night—two of my guilty pleasures. I stared out the window, waiting for Max to come downstairs. He rarely ate breakfast anymore, so I'd stopped fixing anything for him. I didn't know whether or not it was a high school thing or just a Max thing, but I'd decided when the kid got hungry the kid would eat. He was six foot five and two hundred fifteen pounds, so clearly he was eating something. This was something hard for a mother to do—sit back and watch her almost-adult son make choices for himself. Well, maybe it wasn't hard for most mothers, but it had been really hard for me.

I wasn't supposed to have kids. The doctors told me I'd never get pregnant. This was, of course, after John and I tried year after year. And then finally, when we stopped trying, I got pregnant with Max. One of those unexpected blessings.

Two minutes later and right on cue, I heard Max thumping down the staircase. Before I knew it, he'd run over to me and smashed a kiss into my cheek. Max, like his father, was an attractive young man. His high cheekbones, deep dimples, and ocean-blue eyes kept him quite popular with the girls at school. I didn't like it, but the women in my book club found my adolescent son quite the looker too.

"Love you, mom. I gotta run," he said, keys in hand and sprinting toward the door.

"Love you too, son."

And like that he was gone. I waited for him to start his car. John, against my wishes, had gotten him a brand-new V8 Mustang. What teenager needs a car with a 350-horsepower engine? Then he'd souped-up the tailpipes—to help with gas mileage, he said—and I swear you could hear the kid coming from five miles away. Max was a good kid, but peer pressure was hard to resist, even for the best kids. I didn't want to get that call. You know, the call so many other parents had gotten. Or the knock on the door—the one where you knew as you opened it that your child wasn't coming home. Boys and loud, fast cars were sometimes toxic.

It was Wednesday, which meant it was my day to do laundry for the first half of the day and then meet Diane for brunch at one thirty.

I moved from room to room scavenging for clothes, towels, and anything else that needed to be washed. Both Max and John usually did a good job of bringing their clothes down to the laundry room. It'd taken a few years, but I'd finally trained them both. I headed upstairs to do a walk-through, just in case there was a stray here or there. There always was.

John had left a pair of slacks on our closet floor. I picked them up and laughed out loud. Even after twenty years I still had a little more training to do.

Remember, I started this story by saying this was the start to the second-worst day of my life.

As I headed back down the staircase with John's slacks in hand, I checked his pockets, something I always did before washing them. I didn't find the usual spare change or stray business card this time. What I held in my hand was something worse—much worse. It stopped me dead in my tracks.

My pregnancy with Max had been pretty rough. I was put on bed rest the last month, until Max was delivered via C-section. Dr. Lou strongly suggested that I get my tubes tied, which I had. So why was I holding an unused, unopened condom in one hand and an empty condom wrapper in the other? When John and I did have sex, we never used condoms. And we hadn't had sex at all in at least five months.

Suddenly the room was spinning and my head was pounding. I reached out for the banister, but it was no use.

I'd seen people fall down staircases a million times on America's Funniest Home Videos. I never imagined that it hurt so badly.

I was sure that it took less than five seconds for it to be over, but it felt like much longer.

After I reached the bottom, I lay there for a second to try to gather my wits. Everything hurt. My head throbbed. Both of my legs ached, and my back felt like it'd been pummeled with a sledgehammer. I reached up to touch my lips and felt a trickle of warm blood ooze between my fingers. I touched my side and winced; apparently my ribcage had also taken a beating.

Get your shit together, Candice, I said to myself. I lay there another five minutes at least, trying to make sure nothing was broken and that I wouldn't fall again when I tried to get back up. My head was still swimming and I was seeing double. The pants I'd been holding were halfway up the staircase, and the condom and condom wrapper had both made it all the way to the floor.

Slowly, I pulled myself up and tried to shake off the cobwebs. When I got to my feet, I looked over at the mirror hanging in the foyer. I eased toward it, afraid of what I might see glaring back at me. I closed my eyes, willing myself not to look, but then I took a second glance. I swallowed hard and struggled to take a breath. I didn't know if it was from my fall or from the truth that I'd just learned, but the reflection that stared back at me was a shattered one, a jigsawed mirage of a crushed soul, my face a distorted version of what I'd last remembered it to be. My features, no longer defined, had become an abstract joining of pieces.

I stumbled a few steps up the staircase and yanked the pants into my hand, the condom paraphernalia too.

I'd left my cell phone on the table, and I could hear it chiming at me. I had two texts and a missed call, all from John.

I forgot it's laundry day. I'll get the pants I left in the room. Just leave them – I'm sorry still in training I guess. lol

And a second text that read, Did you get my text?

I crashed down into the chair at the dinner table. Out of nowhere, tears started running down my face. I buried my face in my hands and cried until no more tears would come. Then I dry-heaved for another ten minutes, trying hard to catch my breath. How could he? How could I have been so stupid? I didn't need to ask him any questions. Diane was right. She'd probably been right all along. I was the stupid stay-at-home wife and mother watching my piece-of-shit husband come home late every night without questioning a thing. And did that really matter anyway? Would that have stopped anything? Probably not. He'd just do a better job of convincing me that everything was okay.

My eyes still watered. I had so many emotions pouring through me and so many questions. Who was she? How long had this been going on? Did he love her? Was he going to leave me for her one day? Was she younger than me? Prettier? Was it someone he worked with at the office?

Our sex life hadn't amounted to much. I knew that didn't help, but it wasn't an excuse. If he was unhappy, why didn't he just leave? I'd tried to spice it up some. The videos I bought and the sexy lingerie did nothing. I didn't understand at the time, but now it all made sense. And I guess I lied about it doing nothing. It had done something, all right. It'd made John laugh at me and call my efforts silly, which hurt even worse now. It did explain why he cared even less about our sex life now than he had before.

I cried for another hour straight. I picked up my phone at least a dozen times, tempted to call John and tell him what I'd found. Then I thought about Max. Should I tell him? What would he say? I still loved John, but did this mean we were getting a divorce?

Now you should easily understand why this was the second-worst day of my life.

Every couple has secrets that they've stockpiled away. Most of the time it's something trivial: someone spends too much money; someone secretly enjoys singing at the top of their lungs when they're driving to work each day. John spent fifteen years in the military, and I knew there were dozens of things he couldn't tell me. Dozens of incidents that he couldn't or wouldn't even talk about. I understood that, and I'd never pressed him. Some things are better left unsaid. But this was different. This was lies. This was deceit. This hurt. This wasn't Jason Bourne top secret American intel—this was old-fashioned cheating.

I sat at the dinner table for another thirty minutes or so, trying to decide what I would do next. Then I made a choice that I guess, looking back, may not have been the best. I decided I would tell no one. Not John. Not Diane. Not my son. No one.

I wanted to know who this woman was. I wanted to see it for myself. I needed to see it for myself.

I picked up John's pants and put the unused condom and the used condom wrapper back where I'd found them.

John had called two more times, clearly nervous about what he'd left in his pockets. Bastard!

I texted him back with a picture of my face, letting him know that I'd fallen down the stairs but that I was okay. I explained that I hadn't started the laundry and would leave his pants as requested until tomorrow.

I assumed he would at least call to check on me, but he didn't. I got a text back, a simple okay, and that was it. I scrolled back through the photos on my phone and took a second look at the one I'd sent him. My battered face should have alarmed him.

I eased back up the stairs, my back throbbing with each step I took. I tried to arrange John's pants in the closet, just as I'd found them.

Then I fell to the floor and cried for what seemed like an hour. How had we gotten so far apart that it had come to this? Was this all my fault? How had I changed from the sexy woman he couldn't keep his hands off of to the woman he no longer even noticed?

None of it mattered now.

I stood up and looked in the mirror. Stop your damn crying and do something about it, I told myself.

But what was I going to do? Hell, I didn't even know who this woman was. I decided that I would go to lunch with Diane like I always did at one thirty on Wednesdays. I would attend the PTA meeting at Max's school tonight. I would prepare dinner and leave John a plate in the microwave before I headed off to bed. I would leave him an I love you Post-it note on the fridge like I usually did too.

Tomorrow I would find out who this woman was. And one day soon, I would kill her.

Chapter 1

When my dad and I are on good terms, I usually talked to him at least once a day. And every other day, at worst. But I hadn't spoken to my dad in a little over a week, which was odd for me. My parents divorced when I was nine years old. The truth is, they didn't really split; my mom left the three of us. My older sister, Jess, my dad and me. She never called or wrote us, not even on our birthdays or Christmas. I didn't even know if the woman was still alive. We still don't know why she left us. We know it wasn't because of money, because we were pretty well-off. You see, my dad's name is Gus Jones—the Gus Jones. Owner of Calpech Oil and Rigging. The company had just gone public and was valued at almost a billion dollars. So maybe we were a little more than well-off. After high school, Jess (who is two years older than me) and I both attended Texas A&M University, which was our dad's alma mater. We'd both also gotten chemical engineering degrees.

When John and I first started dating, my dad hated him. And now, after almost twenty-five years together and twenty years of marriage, he still hated him. He always said I was too good for John and that he didn't believe John loved me. Until now, I just thought my dad was jealous because I'd found someone. Now I wasn't too sure. The other thought I had was that maybe my dad just wanted me to be more like Jess, who had never married and didn't even have a boyfriend.

My dad had always wanted a boy. He wouldn't dare admit it, but my sister and I always knew that. It didn't bother me; most guys wanted a boy to do boy things with. Dad had tried to do that stuff with Jess and me, until we got to the age where it just no longer worked. He took us fishing and hunting, even taught us how to shoot guns. He coached our Little League sports teams. And we'd played them all—even a year of Little League football. It made us tougher in a lot of ways, I think. And right now, while most women would still be feeling sorry for themselves, maybe my tough, boy-like upbringing was helping me more than ever.

I slowly undressed and pulled myself into the shower. The water made my face sting, and I could feel more cuts and scrapes than I thought I had. As I soaped my body and felt the weight of my breasts in my hands, more tears fell from my eyes. Why had I not been enough for him? I was no longer in my twenties or even my thirties, but I was in shape. I was certain there were dozens of men who would love to jump in bed with me. Or maybe I was kidding myself. Maybe I didn't have it anymore.

After spending forty-five minutes digging through my closet, I finally found what I was looking for. I pulled the skintight, spaghetti-strap, extra-low-cut blouse over my head. As I stared at myself in the mirror, I had second thoughts. What the hell are you doing, Candice? Take it off. You look . . . Well, my double-D breasts filled the blouse and spilled over the top. I didn't know what look I was going for, but I looked good, if I said so myself. Next, I found the tightest jeans I could squeeze into. I'd been a size two when I met John, and now, all these years later, I was right on the cusp of being a size two again, thanks to my trainer, Julian. Close enough that fitting into those jeans was going to work. Barely.

I slipped into my sexiest pair of spiked heels, grabbed my phone, snapped a selfie, and sent it to John.

Heading out to meet Diane for lunch

Usually he only responded back with "K", so I was curious what today's response would be.

Two seconds later, my phone rang. It was John. I decided not to answer. Then, right on cue, I got a text.

Wow you look great – can I come join you for lunch ☺ ?

I replied. Wow back. Surprised you noticed. And no, only girls.

You okay?

Fine. Never been better. About to drive ttyl.

I felt good about letting him see me dressed this way. And now I knew he'd be wondering all day if I'd indeed attempted to wash his pants. Or at least wondering why I'd decided to dress up.

Instead of taking the Acadia today, I decided to drive John's "weekend car," as he called it. It was probably what he drove around in while looking for girls like whoever he'd used that condom with. Had this been a one-time thing with some girl he didn't care about? Or was my husband having an affair? Did he love the woman? I felt tears welling up and fought them off. I didn't want my makeup to run.

I pulled up to Olive Garden and backed the red BMW 440i into a spot. I shut the engine off and climbed out. As I made my way across the parking lot, a car pulled up beside me. A younger man in his late twenties or early thirties had his window down.

"Excuse me, but have we met?" he asked as his eyes wandered over me.

I didn't recognize him, but he was cute and obviously interested. I must admit, it made me feel pretty damn good.

"Umm, no I don't believe so. Unless you're one of my husband's friends. And if so, I apologize."

"Ahh. Husband, huh? That's too bad. I had an entire evening planned for us— the weekend too."

I giggled before I knew it. I could feel my face reddening. "That's very sweet, but yes, I'm married. You have a good day."

As I headed for the restaurant, I listened for the car to drive away but it didn't. I looked back and the guy was checking me out. He stared at me like I was the only woman on the planet. I couldn't remember the last time John looked at me that way. I gave him a sheepish wave and motioned for him to leave, but he just sat there.

"Candice!"

I looked around to see who was calling my name. Diane stood in the doorway, waiting for me.

"Candice! C'mon. Who the hell is that? And what the hell are you wearing? And what the hell happened to your face?"

I glanced back over my shoulder one last time, and the man drove away.

I frowned at Diane, who was still holding the door open. "Clothes, Diane. They're called clothes. And I had a fight with my staircase. It's fine."

"Well, no crap, Einstein. I know they're clothes. But—"

"But what? I felt sexy today, so I dressed like it. Is there a problem with that?"

"No, I don't guess so. It's just strange. I mean, strange for you."

"Why is it so strange? Maybe I'm tired of keeping these things penned up?" I said, cupping both of my breasts.

"Stop that," Diane said, finally smiling.

"No," I said, squeezing them both again. "I kinda like it."

"What the hell has gotten into you? If John see's you out like this . . ."

"What? And besides, he knows already. I sent him a selfie."

A young waitress appeared and seated us.

"I thought you and John weren't even . . . you know."

"We're not. Can you bring me two glasses of whatever wine it is you're serving today?" I said to the waitress.

"So, what's with the—"

"I told you already. I just felt sexy today. Can we talk about something else please?"

"Fine. Michael is going over to check out the new country club this weekend. Is John going with him?"

"I don't know. More than likely."

My mind wandered off. Did her husband know about John's little piece of side ass?

"I don't know. Michael said John's been working a lot more lately."

"Well, he has. So like I said, I don't know. Random question—you and Michael have been married for what, twenty years?"

"Nineteen."

"And he was your first, right?"

"Shhh. Yes."

I looked around. "Why are you shushing me? We're both adults, right? So you're forty years old and have only had sex with one man?"

Diane nodded. "Well . . . I mean, yeah. I guess."

"Well, either you've had more than one penis inside you or you haven't, Diane."

"What the hell is wrong with you today? Did you hit your head when you fell?" She smiled.

"I did hit my head, but nothing's wrong with me. Don't you want to, like, I don't know . . . try something else out?"

"No, Candice, I don't want to try something else out. Geez!" I watched her face flush as she looked away.

"Boring."

"What the hell is this, some kind of midlife crisis or something?"

I laughed. "Maybe. Or maybe I just want to try something new. Does that make me a bad person?"

"Yes. Maybe. I don't know. Why are we talking about this?"

"The same reason we talk about everything, Diane. For the hell of it."

"Speaking of hell. . ."

"What?"

"Did you hear about Maxine?"

"No, but I'm sure you're about to tell me."

"The girl tried to kill herself again."

"You know, I never understood why someone would do that. And what does that have to do with hell, Diane?"

"Well, me and some of the girls were arguing about whether you go to heaven or hell if you kill yourself. And lots of people suffer from depression, Candice. Geez, have a heart, will ya?"

"Hey, I have a heart. My life hasn't always been rosy, but you keep fighting," I said.

"Yeah well, maybe everyone isn't as tough as you. So heaven or hell—what do you think?"

"Honestly, what me or you or anyone else thinks doesn't really matter, does it? Tell you what, when you get to heaven, if you see anybody who killed himself you'll have your answer."

"Me? You're a good Christian woman. You'll be up there right beside me, silly."

"Maybe. If I don't kill a few people first," I said, smiling.

Diane laughed. "Kill someone? You would never hurt a fly. We both know that."

Twenty-four hours ago, Diane's assessment would have been correct. But that was then. This is now.

We spent another hour talking about mostly nothing.

I had about four hours until my PTA meeting, and I still had a lot of questions I needed to answer.

Chapter 2

When I got home, I logged into our cell phone account. If John had been texting or calling this woman, our bill would show it. Then at least I'd have a number and from there I could possibly get a name.

After the page finally loaded, I noticed our account settings had been changed. The detailed listing of contacted numbers on each line was gone. When had he changed that?

I knew what I needed to do next. I reached over, grabbed my cell phone, and unlocked it. Dad answered on the second ring.

"Surprised to hear your voice. I thought you were mad at me."

"Hi, Dad. And yes, I'm mad at you. You're still my dad though, aren't you?"

"Either way it's good to hear your voice. Did you call to tell me that you're getting a divorce?"

"Really, Dad? Can you not be totally impossible for once please?"

"I'm sorry. Can we start over?"

"I need a favor."

"What do you need?"

"Money."

"Money? I thought you and John were doing well?"

"John and I are doing fine. I just need money that . . . no, never mind the details. I really can't talk about it."

"Can't or won't?"

"Both. You gonna loan me the money?"

"I won't loan it to you, but I'll give it to you, sure. How much do you need?"

"Five grand or so will do."

"Five grand?" I could hear the strain in his voice.

"Remember, Dad, no questions. Please. If I'm calling you and asking for five grand—"

"Okay. You want me to wire it?"

"No. Can I meet you in an hour and pick it up from you?"

"Where?"

"The park that you took us to when we were growing up."

"Okay."

"Thank you. And Dad, this is our secret, okay?"

"Got it. You're not in any kind of trouble are you?"

"No. Of course not. I'm fine, Dad."

"Okay. I love you."

"Love you too."

Chapter 3

Tonight was Max's study group night, so I wouldn't see him until later. I'd decided to forgo the PTA meeting after all and find out who this mystery woman was tonight instead. If I'd gone to the meeting I would have just spent the entire night with my mind on her and John anyway.

For once my dad had given me the money and hadn't asked any questions. While it was on my mind, I sent him a text thanking him again. I planned to use the cash to move around and buy whatever I needed without John noticing.

John hadn't been coming home until well after eleven and sometimes as late as midnight. And once he got in, he ate, took a shower, and then came to bed. Most nights I wasn't asleep, only lying there pretending to be. Some nights I wanted him to roll over and hug me, but most of the time I just wondered if Diane had been right all along. The more I thought about it, the more I realized I'd indeed been ignoring all the signs that pointed to infidelity—namely the lack of a sex life, even a bad one.

I called an Uber to take me to John's office. Fifteen minutes after I called, a baby-faced kid driving his mom's minivan pulled up outside our gate. I climbed in and gave him the address. When we arrived, it was four thirty. Maybe John worked with this woman. And if he did, maybe their little fling was happening inside the office. He expected me to be at my PTA meeting, so he wouldn't try to call or text. Typically I wouldn't hear from John until he crept into the house.

Downtown Houston was always going one hundred miles an hour. We parked a half block from the office but close enough to see John's car if he left the parking garage. Tons of cars came and went, making this much harder than the movies portrayed. And a lot more boring.

"Excuse me, ma'am, but are you a cop or something? We on some kind of stakeout?" the Uber driver asked.

I smiled. "Yeah, something like that. You can't tell anyone that you picked me up tonight, okay? It'll be our little secret."

He nodded. "I won't tell a soul."

"I'll throw in an extra twenty when I pay you later tonight. We could be here awhile."

He pointed to the laptop in the seat next to him. "It's okay. You can stay as long as you like. Meter's still running."

Thirty minutes turned into an hour, then two, and soon it was nearing nine p.m. I hated daylight savings time. It put me in a winter funk that I'd never been able to shake my entire adult life. If it got dark on me, I'd have to move on to plan B, which was already in the works. When John did finally make it home, I would turn on his iPhone's tracking feature.

"Almost dark, ma'am."

"I know. We'll wait another ten or fifteen minutes."

Two minutes later, I saw John's look-at-me-yellow Corvette pull out of the parking garage.

I pointed. "Okay, there's our guy. Yellow 'vette. Don't lose him."

"I'll try. But I have to warn you; I've never followed anyone before."

"It's okay, just go. You'll do fine. I'll help you."

I was trying to keep the kid calm, but the fact was, I'd never tailed anyone either. How hard could it be? I asked myself.

We followed John through two lights, and then he merged onto Interstate 45 South. We were three or four cars behind and keeping up fairly well. He wasn't driving fast or crazy, so that made it a little easier.

John had made his way over to the left lane, and we'd been riding there for nearly twenty minutes. The exit to our house was number twenty and was approaching quickly. Could he be going home? How foolish would this all look if it was just some type of misunderstanding? If he was going home, how would I explain not being at the PTA meeting or the Uber? But why would he be going home right now? John hadn't been home this early in nearly a year.

I watched as John's Corvette moved over toward the exit lane. He took exit twenty-three, and we followed him. So it hadn't been some misunderstanding; John wasn't going home. We U-turned under the freeway, and John stayed on the feeder. He made the first right and, a minute later, turned into the Marina Bend apartment complex.

My heart raced. I swallowed hard. The moment you realized that your worst nightmare was actually a reality hurt. It hurt badly, despite my tomboyish upbringing. Damn you, John.

A single tear rolled down my cheek. I quickly reached up to wipe it off and caught the Uber driver eyeing me in the rearview mirror.

"You okay, ma'am?"

I nodded. "I'm fine. Pull up over there." I pointed to a spot about fifty yards away.

We parked in an unlit area of the parking lot. John still hadn't gotten out of his car. My cell phone buzzed.

It was a text from John. I love you

Tears blurred my vision. A minute later, I saw a woman walking down the sidewalk toward John's Corvette. He got out, and the two kissed hard and long for what seemed like forever. We lived less than ten minutes from here. I couldn't believe how brazen he'd been so close to home. I realized that I was shaking. My tears yo-yoed from angry tears to heartbroken ones.

There they were—there she was. Maybe I should just take out my gun and end them both. It'd be called a crime of passion, and they'd let me go with no time. Or maybe I could plead temporary insanity.

I was too far away to tell much of anything about the woman. They were under a lamppost, so I could tell she was blonde like me. And judging her height based on John's, she was pretty close to my five foot six, give or take an inch.

I could see the driver watching me in the rearview mirror. By now he'd probably figured out that I was no cop and this was no stakeout. He didn't say anything to me, which I appreciated.

When John and the mystery woman finished their little greeting, she walked over to a car—hers, I presumed—and took something from the trunk. Then they walked hand in hand out of sight, around the side of the apartment building and, I assumed, into her apartment. I couldn't risk getting out and being seen.

You're probably wondering why I didn't just confront him—her—and just get it all over with. But I wouldn't be able to answer that question anyway.

"I'll be right back," I told the driver.

"Where are you going? What are you going to do?" he asked.

I said nothing.

I walked over to her car and snapped a picture of the license plate. I had a few cop friends, and I'd let them run the plates and tell me who she was.

I pulled up the contact information for one of them and sent a text.

Jeremy, do me a favor. Can you run that plate and tell me who it is please?

He replied less than a minute later. They run you off the road or something? I heard you had road rage issues.

Haha I wish. Send it when you can. Thx.

I'm on patrol tonight and bored out of my mind. This should only take a second. Stand by.

I'd made my way back to my ride and hopped back in.

"Okay. I've seen enough here. Can you take me back home please?"

The kid now had sadness in his eyes. He knew.

"You gonna be okay?"

"Yeah, I'll be fine."

"So are you a PI or something, or was that your—"

"The latter."

We rode in silence for the remainder of the drive.

My phone finally buzzed again.

Lexi Price. 25, no warrants, speeding ticket last year, lives in Marina Bend apartments

Thank you, Jeremy. That's what I needed.

Care to tell me why?

One day soon. Gotta run.

Max got a grown woman stalker or something?

No haha I wish. Really I gotta run.

The car stopped at my house, and I dug in my purse to get his money.

"It's okay. I don't want your money."

I tried handing it to him anyway. "Listen, don't feel sorry for me. I'll be fine. You performed a service, and you deserve to be paid. If you don't take it, I'll just leave it here on your seat anyway. So you really have no choice."

"If you insist."

"I do. Thank you for tonight."

Chapter 4

I went inside, cooked dinner, and ate alone. I poured another glass of wine from what was now a half-full bottle. Some of my hurt was fading and turning into anger. Maybe I wasn't the perfect wife, but I sure as hell didn't deserve this. I'd been sitting at the table a few minutes when I heard the screech of a car's tires. It sounded close, like it was a car leaving my front gate. And it was loud like Max's car, but I knew where he was tonight, so it couldn't have been him. I got up and peered out the window, but all I could see now were taillights. I looked for a second longer, and another car made a U-turn at the gate and headed the same direction as the first car. Maybe it was some silly kids playing car tag. Who knew? I left both John and Max a plate and drew myself a bath. After I undressed and slipped into the warm water, I picked up my phone and went to my Facebook app. I clicked on John's profile and went to his friends list to see if Lexi was one of them. She was.

I clicked on her name and went to her page. I'd always believed that the other woman was just another victim. But suddenly I no longer felt that way. The two of them were Facebook friends which meant, at a minimum, she'd seen his page. She'd seen the pictures of the three of us. In this day and age, there was no way that she didn't know about me and Max.

I trolled the pictures on her page. Most were of her, bikini-clad by the pool or on a boat. So John had gone out and gotten himself a young party girl. I guess I'd gotten too old and boring for him. At least she's pretty, I thought. So many times I'd seen guys cheat on their wives with hideous women, and I never understood that.

Lexi and I weren't Facebook friends, so most of her page was blocked to me. As I put my phone aside and slid deeper into the soothing water, I heard the alarm disarm downstairs.

"Mom, I'm home!" Max yelled.

"Okay, honey. Taking a bath. I love you," I called back. "Food's in the fridge."

"Love you too, Mom, and thanks for dinner."

I finished my bath and headed straight for bed. The warm water had soothed my battered body, but it did nothing to ease my aching heart. Fifteen minutes later, I jumped at the knock on my bedroom door.

"Max?"

"Yeah, Mom, it's me. Food was great. I love you," he yelled through the door.

"I love you too, son. Good night."

"Dad told me you fell earlier. You okay?" he said, cracking the door open.

"I'm fine. Just a little bruised. It's nothing."

He walked over to me. "It looks like a lot more than nothing, Mom. How far up were you when you fell?"

"About halfway. I'm fine Max. Stop worrying."

"Somebody has to worry about you." When the words left his mouth, he looked away from me. A heavy silence filled the room for a minute.

"I'm going to sleep now. Night, Mom. I love you."

He bent over and kissed my forehead and left.

What a sweet boy. Max had always been a momma's boy, which was okay by me. I was sure it drove his girlfriends crazy—which was okay by me too.

I hadn't thought about it before now, but if I left John, what would it do to Max? Max idolized John and this . . . this would crush him. How could John be so goddamned selfish?

I spent the next hour planning what I would say to John when he came to bed and how I would say it.

John, I know about Lexi, and I want a divorce.

He'd pretend to play stupid. His face would wrinkle, and he wouldn't answer me.

How long has it been going on, John?

Again he'd play stupid. Probably say something like, How long has what been going on?

Then I'd ask, Do you love her?

And then he'd go silent.

When you'd been married to someone for twenty years, it wasn't hard to play out a whole ten minutes of dialogue. And to get pretty damn close to how it would go.

I slid out of bed and walked over to my dresser. I eased the drawer open and stared down at my 9mm pistol. I'd backed off my initial reaction, which was to kill the two of them, but only because of Max. I'd put my career on hold to raise Max and get him through school, while John had advanced his career and seemingly left me by the wayside. That made it hurt even more. My marriage was a sham, a hoax, and John and Lexi were laughing at me.

Stupid Candice.

No, not any more. I wanted John to hurt. I wanted Lexi to hurt. I wanted them both to hurt the way I was hurting.

I climbed back into bed and grabbed one of the books on my nightstand. I read until I couldn't keep my eyes open.

I awoke with a start when the security alarm was disarmed two hours later. I heard John stumble into the house. I listened to the beeps as he tried to punch the code into the keypad to rearm the system. It took three tries before he got it right. He—no, they—had probably been drinking. I waited to hear the microwave start up but it never did.

Finally, after ten minutes, I put my robe on and walked downstairs. When I got to the bottom of the staircase, I could see John in the kitchen, staring wide-eyed into his cell phone. I poked my head around the corner. "Still working?" I asked.

John slammed his phone down on the counter and gave me a nonchalant look, as if he hadn't been staring at it like a thirteen-year-old boy getting caught with his first Playboy magazine.

"Uhh . . . yeah. Work," he answered.

"So late? It's almost midnight." I walked closer just to make him nervous, pretending to want a kiss.

He picked the phone up and turned it off.

"Don't stop on account of me. Go ahead and finish. I just wanted a kiss," I said, smiling at him.

John bent down and planted a halfhearted kiss on my forehead. He said nothing about the noticeable bruising from my fall earlier that day.

"No, it can wait till tomorrow. I'm going to take a quick shower before I come to bed."

He walked past me and headed for the staircase. It was faint, but I caught the scent of a woman's perfume. The anger welled up in me again.

"Have you been drinking, John? I thought you had to work," I said, trying my best not to sound accusatory. Trying my best to avoid turning this into an argument.

"Oh, yeah. I took a few clients out to dinner. You know how that goes," he said over his shoulder as he continued to climb the stairs.

"Yeah," I said.

He told me a bald-faced lie right to my face. I don't know why that should surprise me, because John had been lying to me for months now.

I turned off all the lights and then the waterworks began. John was long gone upstairs, so I wasn't worried about him hearing me. It was clear that even if he had, the bastard didn't care about me anyway. Why in the hell had he stayed? Maybe somewhere in all of his selfishness he actually cared about Max and how this would affect him.

After a five-minute pity party, I dried my face and went back upstairs. John was already showered and in bed. Probably knocked out cold from whatever he and Lexi had been drinking. I walked straight to his side of the bed and stared down at him. So many emotions coursed through my veins: anger, pain, distrust, broken promises, regret, more pain, more anger.

Finally, I climbed in bed and scooted as far away from him as I could get. Then I stared up at the ceiling, thinking about everything and nothing all at the same time. I wanted to tell someone, anyone. I wanted to scream. I wanted to grab Lexi by her neck and squeeze the oxygen out of her body, right up to the point where she was about to pass out and then do it again, until I was too tired to squeeze anymore.

I lay there, looking over at the clock every thirty minutes. Three a.m. turned to four and then four to five, and finally, I knew how I would hurt them. I had a plan. On some levels, I wished it was more sinister, but it would be fun nonetheless. And by the time it was over, I'd have both of them eating out of my hands.

Chapter 5

The next morning started off just like every other, despite the fact that I'd only slept about an hour and was dead tired.

After John left for work, I anxiously waited for Max to leave so I could set my plan into motion.

I sat at the table, waiting, and then I remembered I hadn't even made my pot of coffee. I never forgot to make my coffee . . . ever.

The rumbling on the staircase started, and two seconds later there was Max.

"A few minutes early today?" I asked.

"Yeah, well, I wanted to get a look at this face," he said, gently touching my cheek.

"I told you last night. I'm fine. It's nothing, really."

"What happened anyway? I mean, did you just miss a step?"

"Something fell from my hands, and I slipped on it. I'm a little sore. It hurt a lot more than it seems to in the movies."

We both laughed. He hugged me, kissed my forehead, and left for school. Normally I only got the kiss, so falling down the stairs had garnered me a hug too.

I hurried upstairs and got dressed. Ten minutes later, I was on I-45 heading toward Lexi's apartment. I parked in the same spot as the night before. Her car was still there, which was good. It meant she hadn't left for work, which was something that had concerned me.

While I waited for Lexi to appear, I applied for a new credit card online. Something in my own name that I could use for buying things if I needed too.

An hour later, a blonde fitting her description came skipping around the corner of the building. I'd pulled up her Facebook page again and looked down to compare—it was her. I thought maybe seeing her again would evoke some new emotions out of me, but it didn't. The only thing I was focused on now was carrying out my plan and watching them both suffer. The brake lights on her

Chapter 6

I showed up ten minutes later than I'd told Lexi to arrive —on purpose, of course. I wanted to make her wonder even longer who this mystery person was and exactly what they wanted.

When Max was younger, I'd taken him to this park many times. I'd told Lexi exactly which park bench to sit on, as I knew which way it faced. As I walked across the park, I could see a blonde on the bench, her back to me, just like I'd instructed.

She looked like a ball of nervous energy as she glanced one way and then the other, scanning the area in search of the person who had summoned her there.

I slid beside her on the bench. I looked over at her and took off my sunglasses.

"You're a lot prettier than your pictures. I can see why he likes you."

Horror gripped her face.

"Relax. I'm not going to kill you. I mean, don't get me wrong . . . I thought about killing you. And I guess I could at some point change my mind, but for now, no, I'm not going to kill you."

"How did you . . .?"

I laughed. "What did you and John think? That this whatever-it-is was going to go undetected forever? You can't be that stupid. Please tell me you're not that stupid."

I could tell she was afraid, which made me feel good. I knew killing her wasn't in my plans, but what you made someone believe you were capable of was all that really mattered.

"So how long has it been going on?"

She said nothing.

"How long, damn it?" I asked again, raising my voice this time.

"Almost a year," she whispered. "But it's not what you think."

"If you are having sex with my husband, then it's exactly what I think." I shook my head. "Jesus! I can't even believe I'm doing this. Do you love him?"

"I – I don't know. Maybe."

"Lexi, before right now, would you have said you love him? It's a very simple question."

"Well . . . yes, ma'am. I think I love him."

"Don't you 'yes ma'am' me like I'm sixty freakin' years old, Lexi."

"Yes, ma'—I mean, okay."

"You ever shot a gun, Lexi?"

"What?"

"Good Lord, are all twenty-five-year-olds this godammned slow? Does John even hold conversations with you, or is your mouth usually filled with his . . . ? Let me try again. Have you ever shot a gun?"

"No, I don't think so."

"You'd know if you had, Lexi. Why are all of your answers so indecisive? I bet when you're riding on my husband's dick you aren't second guessing then, are you?"

She said nothing. I saw tears well up in her eyes. After a minute she finally spoke up.

"It isn't like that. We love each other."

I laughed again. "Love? You stupid whore . . . you don't know what love is. You think he loves you? He loves putting his slimy little man-piece into you, is what he loves."

She got to her feet. "I don't have to take this."

"Look, Lexi," I said, pointing to the bulge in my pocket. "You see that? Sit your skinny ass down."

She did as she was told and covered her mouth with her hands.

"Yeah, it's called a gun. And you do have to take this. You'll take it and, just like when you let my husband have his way with you, you'll like it. Am I clear? You've got some nerve with your stupid little 'I don't have to take this' rant."

She nodded.

I reached into my jacket pocket and took out two photographs. Both had been printed from Facebook. I handed them to her.

"Your parents and your sister and her kids. You see, I promised I wouldn't kill you. Those people, however—"

"No! Please don't hurt them. I'll go to the—"

"To the what, the cops? I'm the president of the PTA at Clear Springs High School. I'm a member of two local chapters for chemical engineering professionals. Several members of the League City Police Department are personal friends. And what, they're going to believe a skanky waitress who was banging my husband? Please. So, if I see a change in your routine— even one— one of them gets it. Probably start with one of the kids. So if you can take living with that the rest of your life, go ahead." I pointed to her cell phone.

"What do you want from me?"

"Slow down, Lexi. We'll get there. We all past the going-to-the-cops crap?"

She nodded.

"Well now, how often do you see John?"

"A lot. Almost every day."

"Almost every day or every day?"

"Every day."

"I want you to keep seeing him. Keep screwing him too. I'll be able to tell if something changes by his behavior at home. You say something to John and boom . . . one of your nieces gets it. Do you understand?"

She nodded. "You still haven't told me what you want from me."

"Is John giving you money? Sure is a nice apartment complex you live in. Pretty fancy, especially for a waitress."

She sat there fidgeting but didn't respond.

I waved my hand in front of her face. "Hello, Lexi. Can we focus please?"

"He gives me money sometimes, yes."

"What is sometimes, Lexi? Once a week? Once a month?"

"Once every few weeks usually."

"So you just screw him and he gives you my money, huh? You're like a high-end whore, sounds like."

"Your money? You don't—"

I got right in her face before she could finish the sentence. She leaned away from me.

"I'm sorry. We love each other."

I laughed out loud. Then I reined it in before it became uncontrollable. "John did a really good job with you. You're young, pretty, and extremely stupid if you believe that John Harstow loves you. So here's what's going to happen." I reached into my purse for the burner phone I'd purchased and dangled it in front of her. "You see this phone? When it rings, you answer—no questions asked. You're probably making what, fifteen thousand a year, if that, waiting tables? I'll double what you're making. Don't take any more money from John."

"What do I say when he offers it to me? He'll insist that I take it."

"Well, insist that you don't need it. I'll check the accounts too. You're going to become seriously unavailable over the next few months. Starting tomorrow. You're going on a vacation. Three days."

"I don't have money for that. Where the hell am I supposed to go? And what about my job?"

"Call in sick. I'll give you money, and I don't give a damn where you go. Just get the hell out of here."

I stood up and started walking away.

"Wait! What if he, like, tries to come with me? Or won't stop calling or texting me?"

I turned around slowly and lowered my sunglasses just enough that she could see my eyes. "Figure it out or I'll be visiting your niece."

"Hey!"

I'd already started walking, but I stopped and looked back over my shoulder. "Something else you need to tell me?"

"Listen, I'm sorry about all of this, but you really should just leave it alone."

I stared at her long and hard. Then I walked back to the park bench. How could she possibly feel like she was in any position to threaten me?

"Excuse me?" I said, standing directly over her.

She stood up and looked me dead in the eye.

"I said you should go home and forget about all of this. Just leave it alone."

"Forget about it? And what, just pretend none of it is happening?"

"Yes."

I shook my head. "You've got some nerve, little girl. You just remember what I said."

I returned to my car and made it home just in time to beat Max. I took the steps by two, and my body reminded me about my fall the day before. As I slid the gun back into my dresser, the rumbling of Max's souped-up car let me and the rest of the neighborhood know that he was home.

I replayed what Lexi told me over and over again in my head. Just leave it alone. Why in the hell would she think it was okay to tell me that?

Right before the door opened, my feet hit the bottom step.

Max jumped when he saw me. "Mom! You scared me."

"Who, me? Scare a big strong boy like you?" I turned my face sideways, meaning plant one right here.

He obliged, leaning in to kiss my cheek. "How's your face, Mom? And everything else?" he asked with a lopsided grin.

"What did I tell you last night, huh? I'm fine. Just a little scrape. I'm about to cook dinner. Any requests?"

He'd already made it up three steps. "Everything you cook is good, Mom."

I took out some chicken and turned the oven on. I sat down at the table, going over everything I'd told Lexi and everything I planned to do to John.

I dug around in my pocket for my phone and dialed him.

"Everything okay?" he asked, bypassing the standard greeting.

"Everything is fine, John. You working late again tonight?"

There was a pause on the other end. After twenty seconds or so, John answered.

"It's almost four, and I have a huge stack to go through still so . . ."

"Save it for tomorrow. It's not going anywhere, John. Come home and eat dinner with us for once, please." I'd asked John before about forgoing work and coming home early. Each time the idea was shot down, and I'd eventually quit asking altogether.

"I can't, Candice. I'm sorry."

"Can't or won't, John?"

Silence again.

"You know what . . . ? Never mind. See you at midnight."

I hung up, smiling. My only goal was to get John worked up. I didn't really want anything from him right now.

My phone buzzed in my hands.

I'll make it up to you soon.

I read his text over and over again. No, John, I'll make it up to you.

Chapter 7

John Harstow was used to getting things his way. He'd been that way since he was a boy. It was the only thing he knew. His dad had been a prominent business owner, so John had grown up with a silver spoon in his mouth. There was a substantial inheritance that he'd been set to receive when his father passed away, but he never saw a dime.

When John was seventeen, he and his dad got into a huge argument because John got caught smoking weed. It wouldn't have been so bad, but he was also driving drunk—strike three. The police took him home instead of arresting him, and his dad promised to take care of things. A lawyer showed up the next day and helped his dad write John out of his will. Go a year without getting into any trouble, and I'll add you back in, his dad had told him.

Two months later, they found the elder Harstow dead in his bed—cause of death, heart attack. John wouldn't see a dime, not one penny. He watched as his father's estate was divided up by the state and turned over to charity, just like his father had wished.

John spent the next decade-plus serving in the military and left after the secrets and lies became too much for him. Thanks to the GI Bill, John was able to claw his way through college and then law school. He'd met Candice along the way and became more interested when he learned who her father was. There was a time when he thought he loved Candice, but he wasn't really certain. How could one be certain about something so fickle? he'd thought. What he did love was the comfortable lifestyle her father had helped them afford.

The ringer on John's office phone was muted but the red light blinked.

He pushed the intercom button. "What is it, Meredith?" he said to his assistant.

"You have a four thirty with Mr. Abdookie and he's here."

Damn it. He picked up the phone. "Tell him I'm tied up in another meeting, and I'll have to reschedule."

"Sir, you cancelled your last meeting with him and rescheduled for today."

But it was too late; he'd already hung up the phone. Meredith lied to his guest as she'd been instructed to do. Then she went back to the Brad Thor book she'd been reading, as an angry Abdookie stormed out of the lobby.

John picked up his cell phone and sent Lexi a text.

See you in 45 min, leaving the office now

Okay but an emergency came up. Have to leave tonight for a few days. You can go to my apartment and wait. Be there in an hour or so.

What the hell was she talking about? An emergency? Leave town? He'd have to come up with some story for Candice, but he was going with her.

How long will you be out of town?

Few days. We can talk tonight.

Coming with – let me worry about what to tell the wife.

NO. Can we talk later please?

This time John wouldn't respond. What the hell kind of emergency did she have? Something with her sister, maybe? Or one of her nieces? He didn't care. Whatever it was, he wasn't taking no for an answer. He was going with Lexi. No one told John Harstow no.

He dialed Candice and waited impatiently for the call to connect.

"John? You change your mind about dinner?"

"No. Something else just came up. I have to go out of town for a few days. I'll explain later tonight."

There was silence on the line for a second, and then Candice laughed out loud.

"What's so funny?" an agitated John asked.

"Nothing. So, where to, Cowboy?"

"I'll explain when I get home."

He hung up the phone before Candice could ask more questions. What a major screwup, he said to himself. He should've known Candice would ask where he was going.

John reached his car and flung his laptop bag into the tiny back seat.

What the hell was he going to tell Candice about going out of town? That is, if he was going at all, since Lexi had told him no.

After he arrived at Lexi's apartment, he took out two wine glasses. Next, he drew a bath for her and tossed out a few rose petals to make a path to her bed. He'd bought them a few days before and had them hidden in his office closet.

An hour later, and still no Lexi. John was two glasses of wine in and working on a third when he heard a key in the lock.

When the door finally opened, John sat frozen at the island bar, refusing to look up at Lexi.

"Hey," Lexi called out, trying to get his attention.

John said nothing.

Lexi set the shopping bags she was carrying on the table and made her way over to him.

She reached under his chin and tilted his head up to meet her gaze. She glanced down at the wine glass and then over to the half-empty wine bottle.

"Drew you a bath. It's probably cold now," he whimpered.

Lexi shook her head and took the wine glass from his hand. "What are you doing, John? What are we doing?" Tears pooled in the corner of her eyes.

John pulled away and looked at her. "What are you talking about?"

"This. Us. You. Me," she said, reaching for him.

He hadn't seen this coming. "I thought this is what you wanted? No strings attached. No labels. Just fun. Isn't that what you told me?"

She said nothing.

John yanked his arm away from her. "You backing out on me now?"

"You're drunk. You should go home."

"I don't want to go home!"

Lexi took a step back. "Lower your voice please. I don't understand why you're so angry. You have a wife, for God's sake, and a kid. None of this was supposed to happen this way. You know that."

John stared hard into her eyes. "Is that what this is about? My wife and kid? We both knew everything that was at stake when we started this."

"You know what this is about. This isn't a game either of us can win. Goddamn it, John, you know that."

"I don't know anything. You're heading out of town all of a sudden. You told me I can't come. We were supposed to figure it out together."

Lexi laughed.

"So this is funny to you?" he asked.

"Listen to you. You are so selfish. I don't know how I didn't see it before. What if I was seeing someone else? You go home to your wife every night."

"That's not fair. We talked about that."

"No, you talked about it. I listened."

John reached out his hand for hers. She hesitated before taking it. "Come here. I'm sorry. I just . . . I don't want to lose you. Can we start over?"

Lexi said nothing.

John leaned in close and whispered in her ear. "What will they do if I don't see you for a few days?"

Lexi's eyes widened at the memories his words invoked. "I'll deal with them," she said, pushing him away. "I always do."

The burner phone that John's wife had gotten her buzzed in Candice's purse. At first she pretended not to hear it, but then she remembered what she'd been told about answering it when it rang. She took the new phone from her purse. Both of them stared at it. Lexi pulled away from John and tilted the phone so only she could read the text from Candice Harstow.

Be sure he doesn't go with you. Remember what I told you. No funny business or BANG.

John slyly tried to lean over to peek. Lexi backed away.

"New phone? Your weekend getaway?" John asked.

Lexi didn't respond.

"On second thought, maybe I will go home."

He snatched his keys from the countertop and burst through the door, slamming it hard behind him.

Lexi flopped down on her couch and cried. She spent the next forty-five minutes in the same spot. She'd gotten herself into quite a shit storm of a situation. If she wasn't careful, her life and John's—and the lives of everyone they cared about—would be on the line.

Chapter 8

John had sent me a text saying he was on his way home. He hadn't been home this early in at least six months. Probably longer.

John and I had been married long enough for me to surmise what had happened with Lexi.

She told him that he couldn't go. He came unglued. They fought about it. And fearing for her nieces' lives, she held firm. John wasn't used to being told no. He left upset, and now he would be angry the rest of the evening.

I laughed to myself. At first I thought I was laughing to mask my pain. But on second thought, no—this was funny. His text had been short and ill-tempered. He was legitimately upset that his side piece had rejected him.

I lay on the couch reading Jodi Picoult's latest novel and waited for John. I had a slew of questions, but I didn't want to become so inquisitive that John would start to piece things together.

Ten minutes later, I heard his key fumbling in the door. I trained my eyes as hard as I could on my book. How would I have reacted had I not known about Lexi?

I looked up over my book. "Hey!" As soon as the word escaped my lips, I wanted it back. Was hey really the best I could come up with?

"Hey," he replied as he slammed his laptop bag down on the recliner.

"Dinner is almost finished. I made your favorite."

He stared at me with a please stop talking to me look. "Okay."

"Okay?" I really didn't want to fight with John. It took two to get our marriage to this point, and I'd just accepted it for a long time. I certainly didn't want him to question why all of a sudden I was concerned about the way things had been.

He stared at the floor without speaking.

"Do you even remember the last time we had dinner together?" I asked.

"Fine. We'll do dinner."

John was clearly agitated. This Lexi obviously meant a lot to him. A lot more, it seemed, than a booty call. He was seeing her every day and giving her money—my money. He'd been extra short and snappy with me, and I knew when Max came down for dinner it wouldn't change much.

I eased up behind him and wrapped my arms around his waist. I felt his body stiffen at my touch, and he pulled away from me—not enough to break my hold, but enough that I could tell he didn't want to be touched. No, all John wanted right now was his little Lexi.

"Everything okay, hun?" I asked as gleefully as I could.

"Rough day at the office. I'm fine," he said, stepping away from me.

"I'm sorry. You want to tell me about it?"

He turned around and stared at me with a confused look on his face. "Not really."

"Okay. Well, when I have a problem it helps to talk it out. We should talk more often, John. We need to be there for each other."

John continued to stare at me with the most dumbfounded look I'd seen on him in quite a while. I turned away and bit my lip hard to keep from laughing. I didn't know how long I would be able to keep up this little game of mine, but for now I was enjoying the hell out of it.

Before I went to the kitchen to make our plates, I leaned on the banister and yelled for Max to come down for dinner.

"What are you doing?" John asked me.

"I'm about to make our plates. Since you're home, I figured we could actually eat together as a family. You know . . . before you take off out of town."

I could hear Max thumping down the staircase.

"Uhh, about going out of town—"

"Hey, Dad. Who's going out of town?" Max asked as he reached the bottom of the stairs.

"Hey, dear. Your father is going out of town. A business trip?" I said—half question, half statement.

"About that. I don't think I'll be going after all," John muttered.

"You just told me an hour ago you had to—"

He raised a hand to quiet me. "Yeah, well, I was able to get the client on the phone and close the deal. So now there's no need for the trip."

Max eased down at the table. I could tell he noticed the weirdness in the conversation.

"Oh well, that's great. Where would you have had to go?"

John's eyes bore through me. He hesitated before answering. "The client is in Maine."

"Wow, I've never been to Maine. Maybe if things change and you do end up having to go I could come with you. Be good for us to get away for a stretch, like a mini-vacation. Max could hold it down here for a few days without us, right, Max?"

"Well, I am almost an adult now," he said, laughing.

I reached over and grabbed his chin. "Yes, my son, you are."

"Doesn't matter now because, like I said, I'm not going," John said.

I'd just finished setting his plate on the table. I sat down and inched my chair up. "Well, let's plan something else soon. That would make me happy."

John shrugged, not really agreeing with me but not disagreeing either.

"Max, you care to bless the food?"

The three of us endured the most awkward dinner ever. No one said much. I don't think any of us actually knew what to say. It'd been so long since the three of us were in each other's company that we were all, as sad as it sounded, strangers. How could dinner with your husband and son feel so unnatural?

Chapter 9

John sat in the living room, nodding in and out as he pretended to watch an Astros game. I watched as he checked his phone every five to ten minutes. Pathetic. He was still waiting for a text from Lexi. I'm sure he was hoping she'd apologize, tell him she was wrong and beg him to come over. John was longing for a bout of make-up sex that I knew he wasn't going to get. His knees bounced nervously, and he looked more uncomfortable than I'd ever seen him.

"You okay? Seems like something's bothering you."

He shook his head. "Ahh, it's nothing."

"Doesn't seem like nothing. Seems like a whole bunch of something. I'm a good listener. Give me a shot," I said.

"Just work stuff. You'd be bored to death."

I smiled. "Try me. Not much happening around here these days. I could use the excitement."

John stared at me. Was he on to my ruse?

He slammed the remote down on the end table. "Going upstairs. Turning in early tonight. Got a busy day tomorrow, and I need a good night's rest."

I watched John trudge up the stairs, a sad, pouty look on his face. This whole thing would be a hell of a lot easier if we didn't have Max. Divorcing John would crush him. Besides, it would let John off way too easy.

A tear rolled down my cheek and fell onto my book.

"Mom?"

I jumped.

"You okay?"

"Max. Yes, dear, I'm fine. Long day is all."

He crossed his arms and gave me a look that I'd probably given him a hundred times before. Every parent mastered it, the I know something is wrong don't lie to me look.

And now I probably had the look that every kid used regularly. You know it: damn I'm busted I need to come up with a lie really fast.

Think, Candice.

"It's going to be okay. I just found out today that Aunt Janet's mom is really sick," I said. It was lame, but it was all I could come up with.

Next, I got the c'mon mom is that the best you can do look from him. It was all quite comical to me, watching our parent-child roles reverse.

"You sure that's it?"

"Yes. I mean, why would it be anything else?" I forced myself to smile.

"I don't know. Dad seemed kind of weird. I thought maybe you guys were fighting or something."

I nudged him. "Your dad is always weird, isn't he?"

We laughed. "Come here." I pulled him into a tight hug. "Everything is fine."

"I'm going to play basketball for a few hours. I love you."

"I love you too. And be careful."

He looked back at me as he headed for the door. "I'll text you later, but I might spend the night at Junior's house if that's okay."

"Yeah, just let me know."

He closed the door behind him, and I heard the lock snap into place. I felt like a prisoner being locked into a cell. My own little piece of hell.

I spent the next thirty minutes trying to get back into my book, but it was no use. My mind wandered. I couldn't focus.

It had been nearly an hour since John had gone upstairs. By now he'd be fast asleep. I set the alarm, killed all the lights, and made my way upstairs to our bedroom.

John was knocked out cold, just as I'd expected. I tiptoed to the bathroom to brush my teeth. The whirlpool tub looked enticing, but I was just too weary to bother. Instead, I washed my faced, changed into a nightgown, and crawled into bed.

I used my hand to create a thin divide in the sheets—my line in the sand. You stay on your side, and I'll stay on mine.

I lay on my side, facing away from John. The moon sat high in the night sky, and a sliver of light pierced the blinds and sliced across the bed. A chill ran through my body and I shivered. I reached down and pulled the comforter up to my shoulders. I watched the next twenty-two minutes click off my alarm clock.

No matter how hard I tried, I couldn't explain what happened next. A large, gently calloused hand landed on my shoulder. I froze. It didn't take long for me to snap out of it.

"I'd rather you didn't," I said. The last thing I wanted right now was John's hands anywhere on me. He was the reason all of this had happened. I couldn't even remember the last time we'd been romantic. Regardless, it was not going to happen tonight.

I pulled away from his hand and scooted to the edge of the bed. I could feel him inching toward me. He spooned tightly behind me. I could feel his stiffness on me, pressing into my back. I reached behind me and pushed him away. He grabbed my wrist. "Don't pretend you don't want to," he whispered into my ear.

I made one last, weak attempt to pull away from him, but it didn't fool either of us. My body was paralyzed by my emotions. Despite everything my mind was telling me, my body just wouldn't move.

You don't want this, Candice. You don't need this.

But there must have been a part of me that did. A jealous stupidity burned deep inside of me, knowing that, at least for tonight, John wasn't with Lexi. My skin crawled as John's fingers burrowed into my panties and slid them down my thighs. I tried again to push him away, but it was no use. Two seconds later, John was pushing his way inside of me. It had been so long that John felt like a stranger to me.

He grunted and moaned as he moved in and out of me. I felt his hand snake up my nightgown and onto my breast. He kissed and nibbled at my back. I didn't move, but I was no longer trying to push him away. My mind had drifted off, and visions of John making love to Lexi flashed in my mind. A tear made its way down my cheek. "No! Stop." I reached behind me and tried to push John away again.

"What's wrong with you? We haven't had sex in God knows when," John said, finally rolling away from me.

I got out of bed and glared at him. "You've got some nerve," I said. Then I hurried for the bathroom.

"Candice? Candice!"

I didn't stop. I slammed the bathroom door closed and locked it behind me. I leaned against the door and slid slowly to the ground, crashing in a heap on the ceramic tile floor. I lay there and cried until tears no longer came.

Exhausted and spent, I crawled over to the bathtub, put the plug down, and turned on the water. My skin still crawled, and I wanted to wash every trace of John off me.

Chapter 10

"Mom. Mom."

My eyes popped open, and I saw Max standing over me.

"Why are you out here on the couch?"

I was barely awake and trying to get my brain to compute.

"Uh, why am I on the couch?"

"Seriously, Mom?" I could hear the agitation in his voice. I wasn't sure why he seemed so angry.

"It's nothing, Max."

"C'mon, Mom. I'm not ten. If it's nothing, why are you out here? And what does this mean?" He waved a Post-it note in my face.

I reached up and snatched it from him.

It was a note from John. Not sure what's going on. We'll figure it out. I love you, Candy.

Candy. It was a nickname John had given me when we started dating. But he hadn't called me that in five years, probably. Maybe longer.

"Mom?"

I snapped back to reality.

"So you still gonna tell me it's nothing?" Max said.

I stared at the wall behind him. "Max, your father and I have been married for a long time. Sometimes you just aren't in each other's bubble. Like I said, it's nothing. We'll be fine."

I stood up and hugged him. When I let go, Max peered into my eyes. I could tell he was trying to figure out if he should believe me or not.

"I promise everything is okay. You hear me?" I squeezed his cheeks between my fingers.

Finally, he offered up a lopsided smile.

"Now you get out of here before you're late for school."

We hugged again, a little tighter and longer than usual, but he finally let me go and walked out without looking back.

I was starting to second-guess my plan to humiliate John and Lexi. I simply didn't know if I could hold things together long enough. Pretending not to know that your husband was having an affair wasn't as easy as I'd told myself it would be. Max was already on high alert, and if I wasn't careful he'd put two and two together.

It was time for me to set the next step of my plan into action. I'd done some digging online and found a place where you could rent a vehicle for a day completely off the books. As scary as it sounded, I was convinced that with enough money, you could damn near do anything you pleased.

It took me twenty minutes to get to the place. It definitely wasn't in the best part of town. I'd brought my gun with me, but the area still made me nervous. I wasn't even certain I wanted to leave my car here anymore, but following John in my vehicle wasn't a viable option.

I jumped as a tall, slender man knocked on my window.

"Sorry if I scared you," the man yelled through the window.

"It's okay," I mouthed, easing my window down.

"You here to swap out this here car of yours?" the man said, eyeing my car.

"Uh . . . yes, I guess so."

The man leaned into my window. "You got some real spy shit to do or something? That's why most people use us. What, you got you a cheating boyfriend or something? Guy sure would be mighty stupid to be fooling 'round on you," he said, staring down my shirt.

I hit the button on my window and he quickly jumped back. I swung the door open. "I'd rather not say, if that's okay with you. Where's the car?"

He smiled and pointed. "That's her over there."

I squinted at the car. "That thing? Does it even run?"

"Look, lady, you want the car or not?"

"Yeah, I need it. But I don't want to get stranded somewhere either."

"She runs perfect. You wanted something you could blend in with, right?"

He was right. But this car was so far gone, or so it appeared, that I still wouldn't be doing much blending in. It looked like it belonged in a junkyard somewhere, not on the road.

"Keys are in the car. You got the money?"

"Yes." I fumbled around in my purse for the five hundred in cash.

"I'll give you half now and half when I come back for my car," I said.

The man eyed me. "Wasn't the deal, but fine. How long you gonna be gone anyways?"

"I don't know, a few hours. Ad says I can keep it up to six hours, right?"

He nodded.

"I'll have it back by then."

I walked over to the clunker, popped open the door, and climbed in. I was pleasantly surprised by how nice it was on the inside: leather everything, touch screen console, electronic seats—the works. They'd definitely gone to a lot of trouble to beat up the outside of this thing. I fired her up and set off for John's office.

Since I'd found out about Lexi, I'd been monitoring our cell phone records. Of course, I knew Lexi was out of town, but John fielded a two-minute call from an international number that my reverse lookup couldn't identify. The number originated somewhere in Russia, which, oddly enough, was where John had spent the lion's share of his off-the-record military time. Phone calls that lasted two minutes weren't wrong numbers. Telling someone they have the wrong number takes about ten seconds. So who in the hell had he been talking to? I wondered.

When I arrived at John's office, I decided to drive through the parking garage just to make sure he was still there. The people in his office usually went to lunch around noon, and it was a little after ten a.m. He should still be there, but under the circumstances I couldn't be sure. I drove past his car, which sat in its usual spot, and then I parked across the street and settled in.

Time seemed to drag, but I was there for the long haul. I glanced down at the clock on the console: four fifteen. Six hours and, so far, nothing. He'd never even left for lunch. A few restaurants had delivered lunch to the building, so I figured one of them had to have been for John.

Before long Max would be home, and he'd surely text me to find out where I was. I didn't know how long I'd be gone, and I hadn't come up with a plausible story for Max.

Another hour passed with little activity. And then everything changed.

A white van with no markings and no plates pulled up to John's office building. A forty-something man with slicked-back hair climbed out. It was way too hot in Houston for the three-piece suit he was wearing. Maybe he had an interview with someone. The van he emerged from didn't scream "hire me!"

Thirty seconds later, the front doors to the office building opened. It was John. He walked over to the man, and the two began conversing. After a few minutes of back-and-forth, the man followed John inside. Was he one of John's clients? From what I could tell, the man looked like a real slickster.

Eight minutes later—and yes, I was watching the clock like a hawk—the office door opened again, and out came John and the mystery man. The conversation continued, and soon I could tell it had turned south. Both men appeared animated, hands gesturing and heads bobbing as they talked. They pointed in each other's face. I could tell, even from a distance, that their voices had elevated, though I couldn't make out a word of what was said. What were they fighting about?

I sat up in the seat and grabbed the binoculars I'd brought with me. The man shoved John, and he put his hands up. What the hell was this? The man pushed John toward the van. I could tell John was not going willingly. The man yelled something, and John shook his head. Suddenly, the van's back door opened. I fumbled around in my purse for my gun. What the hell was I doing? If these guys were professionals, I didn't stand a chance. They'd gun me down from across the street before I even got the safety off.

I saw an arm reach out from inside the van as the slick-haired man pushed John inside. The door closed and the van sped off. I threw the gun into the seat next to me and slammed the car into drive. The tires squealed as I punched on the accelerator. What the hell was going on? What had John gotten himself mixed up in?

Panic set in. Was this connected to the call he'd gotten? It had to be. Who in the hell were these guys? I called my cop friend and was grateful when he answered on the second ring.

"John's been taken."

Chapter 11

I smashed the pedal on the loaner car as hard as I could. The van had made two quick right turns when it pulled away from the curb in front of John's office. I was losing them. This was nothing like it was depicted in the movies. Keeping up with the van would be nearly impossible in Houston rush-hour traffic.

I realized I still had the phone up to my ear.

"Jeremy, did you hear me? Someone took John."

"Candice, slow down. You're making no sense. Who took John?"

"Damn it!"

"What? Damn it what?"

I slammed on the brakes and pulled the car over to the side of the road. The van—John—was gone. A streak of fear zipped through me.

"Someone came to John's office. They were outside talking, and the guy pushed him into a van and sped off."

"Wait . . . and you just happened to see this?"

"It's complicated."

"Well, if you want my help, uncomplicate it for me. You called a few nights ago asking me to run a plate and now this. You aren't leaving me much of a choice here."

He was right. I was talking to a cop. What had I really expected?

"John's been seeing a girl named Lexi. I found some things in his laundry a few days ago that made me suspicious. I followed him to her house a few nights ago. That's whose license you ran for me the other night."

"God, Candice. I'm sorry. I had no—"

"I know you didn't. No need to apologize."

"So fast-forward to today. Tell me what happened. And try not to leave anything out."

I ran Jeremy through my morning and what my plan had been, up to the point where John was pushed into the van.

"So there you have it. I don't know who those men were, but it wasn't a friendly visit. I could tell that much."

"I'll put a trace on his cell phone. If these guys are professionals, I'm sure it was tossed out the window along the way. But it's worth a shot."

"Thanks. This is going to sound strange, but could we keep this just between us?"

"Candice! I have to make some noise here, or you might not see John again."

"No. Please. They wouldn't have left so many loose ends if they were going to kill him. Taking him in broad daylight in front of his office building?"

"I hear you, but it's risky. Really risky. You're asking me to pretend I don't know my friend's been kidnapped. To just sit on it. How long are you expecting me to wait, Candice?"

"I'll call you back."

I ended the call and set my cell phone on the console. I looked up to find a homeless man hobbling in my direction. When he banged on my window, I reached over and buzzed it down without thinking. Before I could speak, he lunged for me. He whipped a white rag from his pocket and smashed it over my face. I scratched his arms and tried to pry the rag from my nose, but it was no use. As my strength drained away, the man reached into the window with his other hand, grabbed the back of my head, and slammed my face into the steering wheel.

Chapter 12

I woke up to the sound of unfamiliar voices speaking a language that I didn't recognize. The lights hurt my eyes, and I quickly shut them again. My mind raced as I tried to make sense of it all. I could feel sweat pouring from my skin. Who had taken me? Would they go for Max too?

My head pounded, and I could feel a knot on my forehead. I looked around the nearly empty room to try to figure out where the hell I was.

As I tried to sit up, I realized that my hands were bound—my legs too. I tugged on my restraints, but it was no use.

"She's awake," I heard one of the men say.

"Who are you? And where the hell am I?" I said.

"We'll ask the questions here. What do you know about Klondike?"

I shook my head, and the movement nearly made me vomit. "What?"

"So you want to play games, Mrs. Harstow?" the man asked, waving my driver's license.

His accent was thick and heavy. The man was Russian.

"I promise I'm not playing any games. I don't know anything about Klondike—what it means, what it is, or anything else."

The men laughed. "You are John Harstow's wife. After all these years, surely he has told you something, no?"

These had to be the same men who had taken John.

"I swear I—"

Suddenly, the door burst open. "She doesn't know anything," a woman said as she barged into the room. The door was behind me, and I couldn't turn my head far enough to see who the woman was, but I didn't recognize the voice.

"I told you to just go home and leave it alone, Candice."

I yanked hard at my restraints again as the woman—Lexi—came into view.

"You!" I seethed.

"I couldn't have been any clearer, Candice. Now look at the mess you've gotten yourself into."

"Who the hell are you? And what do you want from me?"

"I don't want anything from you. Remember, I told you to leave it alone. We don't have a problem with you . . . or at least we didn't. Lou and Ricco here picked you up because you were snooping around, playing cops and robbers. They had no idea who you were."

"Well, excuse me for following my cheating husband to see what he was up to."

The men's eyebrows raised. "What cheating is she talking about, Nika?" one of them asked.

"I'm not sure, but none of this has anything to do with our operation. Why did you bring this woman here? Now we have no choice but to kill her."

Nika? I thought to myself. And she knew one hundred percent what cheating I was talking about. But I decided to keep that to myself for now. The only thing I needed to focus on was saying whatever it took to get out of this alive.

"No."

"No?" Lexi said.

"No, you can't just kill me."

"Yes, we can. Take her out back and put two in her skull," she told the men.

The goons moved toward me. "No. I mean, I was talking to a cop when he came to my window, before they took me."

All three of them laughed. "Very clever, lady," one of the men bellowed.

"Check my phone. I'm telling the truth. One of my good friends is a cop—Jeremy Girling. I called him when you took John."

They stood there staring at each other, trying to decide if there could be any truth to what I'd just told them.

"Check it out," Lexi barked at them.

One of the men pulled my phone from his pocket. A minute later, I heard the clicking of computer keys. Lexi eased over to me and bent down close to my face.

"One more word about John cheating to these guys or anyone else, and the next time these guys pick you up it won't end well. Nod if we see eye to eye."

I turned away from her and nodded.

"Oh, and if John makes it back home, be sure not to mention this to him either. Got it?"

So basically she was telling me I had no options. I was just supposed to pretend the last hour of my life had never happened.

"This isn't complicated, Candice." She pulled a phone from her pocket and showed me a picture of Max from my Facebook page. "Payback's a bitch, aint it?" she whispered to me before walking away to join the men.

One of the men pointed to the computer monitor. "Looks like what she's saying is true, Nika. She was talking to a goddamn cop."

"It's fine. Blindfold her and drop her ass off somewhere."

"Where you want us to take her, boss?"

"Damn it, Ricco, I really don't care. Just make it a clean drop. Can you handle that?"

Lexi winked at me and waved as she headed for the door behind me.

"Wait. What about John?" I asked. "What are you going to do to him?"

I heard the door open and close. Lexi had left without replying.

"Sorry about this, but we gotta do it," the man named Ricco said as he neared my face with another white rag in hand.

Chapter 13

I felt the weight of a fat-fingered hand on my face. "Hey, lady, wake up!"

I opened my eyes to darkness and realized I was still blindfolded and bound. Where the hell had they taken me?

"Listen, I'm going to cut you free. You count to one hundred before you take that blindfold off, though. You hear me?"

I nodded.

"I ain't playing, lady. You seem real nice, but I'll shoot you right here."

I nodded again. "I understand."

"For Christ's sake, Ricco. Hurry up!"

"Shut up. You can't rush perfection. And besides, Nika told us not to mess this up. And I really don't want to have to shoot this nice lady."

He squeezed my wrists together, and I felt the binds release as he sawed them off. I rubbed my wrists to get the blood circulating again.

"Remember what Nika said. You never seen us, talked to us, or anything . . . or we're coming back. We know where to find you."

I nodded again. He dropped my phone onto my lap. Ten seconds later, I heard two car doors open and close, and the vehicle screeched away. I started counting in my head, as instructed. I had an urge to yank the blindfold off my head right there and then, but these guys seemed serious.

Even after I finished counting to one hundred, I just sat there for several moments. The reality of it all was quickly sinking in. I wasn't sure who Lexi—Nika—was, or Klondike, or what they were going to do to John, but it was clear we were both in deep now. And whatever it all meant was of the utmost importance to some dangerous and deadly people.

Lexi had told me to keep my mouth shut, which meant I couldn't even talk to John about it if they let him go. How the hell could I pretend that I hadn't watched him get taken, that I hadn't been drugged, abducted, and released? But Lexi had threatened Max, so my lips were sealed.

I had way more questions than answers. Everything was a blur. John was working with the Russians. Was he a spy? Was he being coerced, forced to do things against his will in order to keep Max and me safe? Was this why he'd been spending so much time with Lexi? Was this how the affair started?

I had no answers. I took off the blindfold and got to my feet. I was in a park somewhere. Using my phone, I pulled up my location on a map. If it was accurate, I was about a one-hour walk from the loaner car and John's office. At the moment, I didn't have the energy to walk that far. On top of that, my purse was missing. I wondered if it was still in the loaner car. And what about the car keys? It was highly unlikely that the car would even still be sitting there.

So here I was, an hour away from the car, with no money to pay for a cab or an Uber. And any friend I called right now would no doubt ask how the hell I wound up here. And why the hell I had a beat-up loaner car to begin with. And why I had a huge knot on my head . . . and, and, and.

No choice, Candice. Suck it up and get your feet moving.

I set off on foot toward downtown. Texas heat was unforgiving, and today's ninety-five degree temperature was unbearable. How in the hell did Max and all those other boys play football in this? And in pads too.

Sweat poured from my head and ran down my face. I swiped my hand across my eyes and blinked back the salty sting.

I thought back to the last few months. Nothing stood out to me, other than John not being home, and I'd attributed that to work. It was certainly nothing new. But John was in some kind of trouble. Serious trouble. Was the military involved? Had John double-crossed the Russians? My thoughts were all over the place.

I finally reached the spot where I'd been taken and was relieved to find the loaner car still there. I yanked the door open and slipped behind the wheel.

I leaned over and opened the glove compartment. Much to my surprise, my purse was still there. Houston's crime rate wasn't as bad as some U.S. cities, but it was bad enough. This was truly a gift.

I flipped open my wallet and counted out a few thousand dollars. The cash my dad had given me would again come in handy.

I pulled the loaner car back into the driveway where I'd picked it up hours earlier. I killed the ignition and waited.

The front door flew open, and the man who had loaned me the car stormed out.

"Where the hell you been, lady?" he said. "It's been—"

"Long story. Here's some cash." I handed him a wad of money—two thousand dollars. "Do you think that'll cover it?"

He rifled through the stack of bills, wide-eyed, before handing me my keys.

"Let me know if you need to borrow her again, ma'am," he said with a toothy grin.

"Let's hope that won't be necessary."

With that, I jumped into my car and sped away.

Chapter 14

I got home forty-five minutes before Max was expected home. Enough time to start dinner and clean up some. And to have a glass of wine or two.

As I walked past a mirror in the living room, I hesitated. I waited for a split second and then took a step back. The reflection I saw looking back at me stopped me cold in my tracks. It was like a mosaic, fractured pieces of my face, as if the mirror itself was broken. I guess my whole life was like that right now, a beautiful mess of different pieces that barely touched.

How in the hell have you gotten into this shit, Candice?

It wouldn't be the last time I asked myself that question. I was sure of it. As mad as I was at John, I still feared that I might never see him again. That I may never get answers to all of my questions. The more I thought about it, I realized the John I knew had left months ago, maybe even before that. And what kind of danger were we all in?

When people talked about their marriage falling apart or falling out of love with someone, it was never an overnight thing. As I looked back and reflected, John's withdrawal from our marriage, from my life and Max's, happened slowly. In the beginning he would miss dinner once a week, and then that turned into two dinners a week. We'd always had date night on Saturday nights, but that eventually stopped too. He forgot our anniversary, and he even forgot Max's seventeenth birthday. Working late, he'd said. All things seemingly replaced by his relationship with Lexi. And loneliness was my next-best friend.

And through it all, I stayed the course. I forgave and forgot—again and again and again. Maybe it was easier to pretend that everything was perfect. Wine and books had become mainstays. I thought I'd miss the sex, and initially I did, but eventually I didn't miss that either.

I plopped down on my bed and tried to decide what my next move should be. Everything inside me was telling me to at least let Jeremy know what was happening. But Lexi had made it clear that my life and Max's were on the line. Unlike our first meeting, she'd exuded a confidence that made me believe she was more than capable of everything she'd promised.

I heard the front door rattle open.

"Mom? Mom, you home?" Max yelled at me from the bottom of the staircase.

"I'm here, Max," I hollered back to him. "I'll be down in a few minutes. Dinner will be ready in twenty."

I hurried to the bathroom, grabbed a wash rag, and scrubbed the sweat and smeared makeup off my face. I took a deep breath, determined to forget about what'd happened earlier and focus on Max.

"Mom?"

"Coming," I said, heading down the stairs with a fake smile on my face.

"Mom, have you heard from Dad?" Max asked without looking up from a paper he was holding.

I swallowed hard. "No. We haven't spoken in a few hours. What do you need with him?"

Max shook his head. "I've called and texted twenty times at least. We've got our first practice tonight from six to ten, and Coach wanted to go over some plays that Dad said he drew up." He looked at me and cocked his head. "You've got a lump on your forehead. Did you fall again, Mom?"

I laughed it off. "No, silly. It's just left over from the other day. And as for your dad, he's probably just busy in meetings. You know he wouldn't miss your first day of practice for the world."

Max picked up his backpack and trudged up the stairs. He stopped midway. "I used to believe that, Mom. But the way Dad's been acting lately, I don't know."

Kids are much more perceptive than we want to give them credit for. Max had never said a word about John's behavior, but at least now it was clear that it hadn't gone unnoticed.

While I cooked dinner I played everything over again and again in my head. If they hurt John, or worse, any half-witted detective would end up at John's office. His truck was still there. They'd ask employees, who would report that he'd been missing all day. Any CCTV recordings in the area would show my chase and subsequent abduction. It would all come out.

Just then my cell phone rang. I didn't recognize the number.

"Hello?"

"Candice, it's me. John."

I froze. I hadn't been expecting a call from him, at least not so soon. I said nothing.

"Candy?"

"Sorry. I'm here. You okay? You sound out of breath."

"Me? Yeah, I'm okay. Had an off-site meeting with a customer and left my darn cell here on my desk."

I didn't respond.

"I noticed that Max texted and called a few times. Everything okay at home?"

I could hear the stress in his voice. "First football practice is tonight. You were supposed to have—"

"Crap! I was supposed to meet with Coach Blaslins. Damn it. What time is it? I've still got time. I'll leave now."

"Are you sure you're okay, John? You sound . . . I don't know . . . worked up."

There was a long pause on the other end of the phone. "Rough meeting earlier today. We're on the verge of losing a huge client. One that we can't afford to lose."

I paused and then finally spoke up. "I'll see you when you get home, John."

"I love you, Candice."

"I know, John. See you soon."

Chapter 15

Nika stared at her phone, scrolling through her Facebook page as she waited for their leader to arrive. He rarely made a trip to the States, and neither Nika nor her comrades had any idea why he was coming. He'd always told them that the risk was too high. All trips would be on an as-needed basis. So why in the hell was he needed here now?

And why had he wanted to meet with each of them separately?

Her phone buzzed—a text from Ricco letting her know that the boss had arrived.

Nika waited.

Forty-five minutes went by before the door finally opened. She hurried to her feet and rushed over to greet him.

Alexander Prodinov was a physically imposing man who stood just a shade over six foot four. And despite being almost fifty years old, his physique was equally as impressive. Prodinov was a proclaimed fitness junky and it showed.

He reached out his massive arms and bent down, turning each cheek for Nika to kiss. Two of his bodyguards stood behind him. He sat down and then gestured for Nika to do the same.

Nika didn't know why, but she was nervous. Prodinov had never traveled this far without a good reason. Being the head of the Houston chapter of Prodinov's gunrunning operation wasn't an easy job, especially when working part-time as a waitress as her legit cover.

Prodinov laid two fingers on his pursed lips and studied her. "You must be wondering why I am here."

"Yes. I mean, a little. I thought operations were going well."

"For the most part, they are."

"What do you mean by 'for the most part,' Alexander? I have done everything you've asked. We are making a—"

He put a hand up and smiled. "Business matters are fine, Nika. The information flow from the American has been disappointing, however."

They glared at each other.

"He provided you with many details, no? Lots of good intel," Nika countered.

"In the beginning, yes, that is true. But lately I have seen nothing new, and this troubles me. I fear you may be losing him."

"Alexander, the target is still under our control. You must have faith in me. He has to obtain the information without leaving a fingerprint. The technology America uses to guard its secrets requires time and a high level of skill."

"Do not lecture me, Nika. I am well-aware of what Americans can do with technology. There is high risk with this operation for what has lately been little to no reward."

"I wasn't lecturing, and I understand. How much time can you give me?"

"Not long, or this contract may expire soon," he said in a tone that made the hairs on Nika's neck bristle.

Nika froze. "Expire? What does that mean?"

Again Prodinov smiled. "Some of the men believe you have lost your fire for Russia."

"That's nonsense. I've risked my life for many years here in America."

He stared hard at her. For a man in his position, loyalty was of utmost importance. And he had no problem eliminating someone the instant he felt their loyalties wavering. It was how he had ascended so quickly and how he'd stayed at the top so long. If you crossed paths with Alexander "The Czar" Prodinov, you were never seen or heard from again.

Disgust, anger, fear, and confusion all jumbled in Nika's brain, and it showed.

"Alexander, you know I appreciate everything you have done for me and my family."

"I'd like to think you have earned those things. But now I wonder. I've heard things, Nika. My team is looking into several of your affairs."

She swallowed hard. "I have nothing to hide. I would never betray you."

"Then you should have nothing to worry about. All of this can be ended if more info—"

Nika's face reddened. "More? I have spent nearly a decade providing you information. I have proven my value time and time again. How long must I continue to prove myself?"

Prodinov smiled. "Maybe my intel was wrong. Must I remind—"

She fell to her knees in front of him. "No. I'm sorry for speaking out."

"Rise and take your seat, Nika. I admire your passion. However, see to it that it is not misplaced."

He stood, walked toward the door, and whispered something to one of his bodyguards. The man looked up at Nika and smirked.

After the men left, she hurriedly unlocked her cell phone and typed a text to her informant-lover.

Trouble brewing need to meet now.

Chapter 16

I heard a car door slam and rushed to the foyer to let John in. Despite everything that was going through my mind, I was still relieved that he was home.

I could feel the color drain from my face when I saw Jeremy standing there.

"You going to invite me in or just let me stand here?"

"Come in, silly. I just wasn't expecting you."

"Well, that couldn't have been any clearer," he said, reaching out for a hug.

"I'm sorry. Things have been a bit crazy the last few days."

"That's why I'm here. Mind if I sit down?" He gestured toward the couch.

"Not sure if now is a good time," I said, pointing upstairs.

"Candice, if you don't tell me what's going on it's hard for me to help."

Jeremy sat down on the couch anyway. I guess it was his way of telling me that we were indeed going to talk about it.

"Max should be down in a second. Wait till you see how tall he's gotten. And John should be home any minute now. I'm sure he'll be happy to see you too."

"Happy to see me? Why? You know John and I aren't anywhere close to being happy to see each other."

"Despite what craziness you think John may have been involved—"

And then it hit me. Jeremy had confronted John a few months earlier, questioning what he considered sketchy activity that someone had tipped him off about. Something else that John had a quick, reasonable explanation for. Something else that I'd brushed off.

"You were saying?" Jeremy said.

I heard Jeremy talking to me, but I wasn't there. He waved his hand in front of my face, "Candice?"

"You are still Max's godfather, and this family will always love you," I finally offered up.

Almost simultaneously, Max came storming down the staircase and the front door opened again. This time it was John.

I've been involved in my share of awkward moments. This one was right up there with the best of them.

Max was well-aware that John and Jeremy were at odds. He stared at John, who stared at Jeremy, who stared at me. No one said a word. We'd all been frozen by the moment.

Finally, after what seemed like forever, I broke the ice. "Max, aren't you going to say hi to your Uncle Jeremy?"

He traipsed over to Jeremy to exchange a hug.

John gaped at me. "Why is he here?" he mouthed. I shrugged and turned away from him.

"You here to apologize, Jeremy?" John asked.

Jeremy smiled. "And how the hell are you, John?"

"Never been better. You didn't answer my question. If you aren't here to apologize, I'd like you to leave."

"C'mon, Dad. Can't you two put whatever it is behind you?" Max pleaded.

"I wish we could, son. But sometimes things are said that you just can't get past."

"It's okay, Max. I probably should have called before I showed up. You guys start football tonight, right? First practice? Just came by to wish you well and pray over your session."

John rolled his eyes.

"Yes, sir. I'm glad someone remembered that today is my first practice," Max said, cutting his eyes at his dad.

John's eyes burned through Jeremy and then darted over to Max.

He managed a smile, but I could tell it was forced. "Wouldn't miss it for the world, son. That's why I came home early today. I'm going to ride up there with you and have that meeting with the coach."

"I've been texting you all day, Dad."

"I had an off-site meeting with a big customer. I ran off and left my phone on my desk. I'd never forget about something as important as this."

Max rolled his eyes and headed toward the staircase. "I'm going to finish getting ready, Mom. Good to see you, Uncle Jeremy."

After Max pounced back up the stairs, the awkwardness that had flooded the room moments before reared its head again.

John walked over to the front door and opened it. Jeremy stared at me, waiting for me to help soften the situation. I had no words to offer.

"Jeremy, you're Max's godfather, so one day, if only for his sake, I'd like to put this behind us. It's going to take some time. The things you accused me of . . . No need to rehash it," John said, still holding the door open.

As Jeremy strode toward the door, the two old friends never took their eyes off each other. When he finally reached the doorway, Jeremy paused and took a glance back at me.

And then he was gone.

Chapter 17

John Harstow sure as hell hadn't imagined that his life would end up like this. He'd spent years in the military learning about different types of espionage. He knew this lifestyle was much like being a drug dealer, meaning it could end only one of two ways—dead or in jail. The Russians had known exactly which buttons to push, and once he caved a little they pounced, driving the wedge deeper and deeper into his life.

John didn't know how Jeremy had found out, what had tipped him off, but he'd been right. It only made John angrier at his longtime friend.

And now, despite everything falling apart around him, he was back at Lexi's apartment like a lovesick puppy, waiting for her to arrive.

He twirled the wine around in his glass and stared down into it, as if it was going to give him the answers he needed.

The door opened and Lexi—Nika—walked in.

They shared a long embrace and an even longer kiss, one that neither of them wanted to end—ever. Finally, John pushed her away and the pair stared into each other's eyes.

"Didn't think we'd ever wind up here," Nika said, her eyes filled with tears.

John laughed. "You're young. And when we started, you were even younger and more impressionable. Way too young to have been asked to come here and do what you have. But that's why it worked too. No one suspects a fourteen- or fifteen-year-old high school girl to be working for the other side. It's brilliant, actually. Sinister but—"

"I did what I needed to for my family. Maybe if my brother hadn't gotten into all of the . . . It doesn't matter now. I was old enough to know better when things started getting serious between us. I was twenty-three. And I knew you were a married family man."

"I don't even know—"

She placed her finger on his lips. "Like I said, none of it matters now, my love."

"So do you really think Prodinov knows? How sure are you?"

She stared up at him. "I've known him as long as I can remember. He is the smartest man I know. Traveling here from Russia is risky for a man like him. One mistake, even if he's not the one to make it, could spell disaster. The Czar doesn't risk coming here unless something is terribly wrong and in need of intervention. And he only gives termination orders in person."

"So . . . what, he traveled here to—"

"He never orders a kill unless he can look into the person's eyes. He says he can always tell when someone has double-crossed him. He hasn't lasted this long without being right most of the time."

"But—"

"But what, John? He's right again. I've been able to fool so many people during my time here in America. I pull my low-cut shirt down a little, smile and wink, touch a man's arm just right, and I get everything I want. With some people, a little pout of the lips and some serious eye contact is enough. Knowing what's at stake, I don't feel like I was able to fool The Czar."

John tucked a finger under Lexi's chin and tilted her head up until their eyes locked. "Maybe you did enough."

"Maybe I didn't. I think it's time that we do something we haven't done in a long time."

John's eyes widened. She hesitated for a second and then slowly pushed him away.

"Yeah? And what's that?" he asked.

"We need to figure out how we want this to end—for both of us. For God's sake, John, you still have your wife and son to think about. I never wanted anything to happen to them."

John took Lexi's hand and moved it toward him until it rested on his Glock.

"You feel that? We'll be fine. I've dealt with guys like him before."

Lexi shook her head. "No. You won't be fine, and neither will your family. It's difficult to shoot an enemy that you don't see coming, my love. And trust me, you will never see them coming. You won't know you're in their crosshairs until it's too late—if ever."

John stared at Lexi. Anger flashed across his face. He clenched his fists.

"So that's it? You're just giving up? No fight in you? I've risked everything for you—for us."

Lexi took a step toward John.

"You aren't the only one who's given something up here. What do you think they'll do to my family back home? To me?"

Their silence was deafening.

"Come here," John said, reaching out for her. For five minutes, they clung to each other, neither of them saying a word.

"Quite the mess we have here, huh? It was fun though, wasn't it?" he said, forcing a smile.

Lexi's smile was just as hollow. "Yeah, it was. I had some good times with you, John Harstow."

"So what now? I don't know if I can just turn around and walk out that door."

"I don't know what you want me to say. Maybe I'm wrong about why Alexander is here. If I am, and we get a second chance . . ."

"What? If we get a second chance, what?" John asked.

Lexi stroked John's face with the back of her hand. "You were always a little more handsome when you were upset. I never told you that before."

John stepped back. "If we get a second chance, what, Lexi?"

Lexi stared hard into John's eyes. "If we get a second chance, we need to be smarter than we were this time."

"I agree. But what does that mean to you—be smarter? Be more careful of how I come and go?"

She shook her head and took a step back. "No. If we get a second chance, there won't be any come-and-go, John. Like I said, we need to be smarter."

Lexi stood on her tiptoes and kissed John on the forehead. "You'll always have a place in my heart," she whispered.

A tear rolled down her face, and he gently wiped it away. Tears welled up in John's eyes too. Without looking back, Lexi walked into her bedroom and closed the door.

And just as quickly as it had begun so many months before, it was over.

Deep down, John knew it was true, but he stood right where Lexi had left him, paralyzed by the finality of it all. He looked over at the door and waited. One minute, two, three . . . but the door never reopened. Finally, fifteen minutes later, he grabbed his keys and left.

Chapter 18

2 weeks later...

A couple weeks had gone by and things were starting to feel normal again around the house. The new normal we'd all come to accept. John was no longer "working late" or staring at his phone waiting for it to chime.

Max's senior year of football was full steam ahead, and we were one day away from his first scrimmage. He and John had started bonding again. They'd been lifting weights together in the garage and playing catch in the backyard, which made me smile when I spied on them from the window.

After a few days of getting over that season of his life—our lives—John seemed at home again. And not just in the physical sense. It felt good. I hadn't realized how much I'd truly missed him.

We never talked about Lexi or either of our kidnappings. We both just somehow pretended that nothing had ever happened. John was smart enough to know I knew something, but he never asked and I never offered. For the sake of our relationship, we had, in a sense, let bygones be bygones.

The back door flew open and Max bolted in. "Going for a mile run, Mom. Care to join me?" he said with a smile?

I shook my head. "No way an old lady like me could keep up with you."

"C'mon, Mom. I'll go slow."

I walked over to the front door and opened it for him. "I don't think you can run that slow, son."

"Okay," he said as he headed out. "Last chance."

I shook my head again.

As I pushed the front door closed behind him, John strolled in through the back door. We looked up at each other and our eyes locked.

"Feels good, doesn't it?" he said, walking toward me.

I still wasn't one hundred percent over it all, and I didn't know if I ever would be.

Finally I offered a feeble smile. "It feels okay, I guess."

"Just okay?" he said, grasping my butt with both hands and picking me up.

John hadn't picked me up like that in years. I was a little surprised that he was still able to lift me.

He spun us around a few times, and when we finally stopped, he kissed me. I hesitated at first, but it didn't take long for me to give in. I felt my arms tingle with goosebumps.

Suddenly, we heard a knock at the door. We stared at each other for a second, apprehension clouding our eyes.

"You expecting someone?" I asked.

He shook his head and headed over to the door.

John opened it to find two men standing there, both wearing nice suits and serious expressions.

"John Harstow?" one of the men said, flashing a badge.

"Yes. Is there something wrong, sir?" John asked.

"I'm Detective Jones, and this is my partner, Detective Porter. May we come in? This should only take a few minutes."

John paused for a moment, mulling it over, and then gestured for the men to come in.

"You can take a seat there." He pointed to the love seat.

John and I sat on the couch. No one said a word at first; we all just stared at each other.

"What's going on, detectives?" I finally asked.

"Mrs. Harstow, I presume?" Detective Jones asked.

"Yes. You want to tell us what's going on here?" I repeated.

The other detective, Porter, cleared his throat. He handed John a picture. "Mr. Harstow, do you know the woman in this photo?"

John took the picture and looked down at it. He paused for a long moment, saying nothing.

"Well? Do you know her, Mr. Harstow?" he asked again.

John shook his head. "Can't say that I do, detective. I'm sorry I can't be of more help."

I only looked at the picture for a second, but I saw all that I needed to see. Lexi lay dead with a bullet wound to her forehead and one to her abdomen.

I'd never had any run-ins with the police, but I knew that lying to detectives usually didn't end well. And there was obviously a reason why they were here asking John questions about a dead person. I can't say that I would've answered any differently, but this wasn't good. Why had someone killed her, and why did they think John had something to do with it?

"Again, I'm sorry I can't help you, gentlemen," John said, handing the photograph back to the detective.

"No, you keep that. Look at it again. We need you to be sure that you don't know her," Jones said.

"I've taken a nice hard look, and I'm sure I don't know the woman."

Jones handed John a few sheets of paper. "That's a copy of this woman's cell phone records. Take a look at those circled numbers. You recognize that number?"

John looked at me and then down at the papers he was holding. He said nothing.

Jones spoke up again. "Well, Mr. Harstow? Any explanation why a dead woman that you don't know would've been blowing your phone up day after day? And notice the length of those calls. Three minutes, five minutes. Wrong number phone calls don't last one minute. Would you care to look at this picture again?" He dangled the photo of Lexi in the air.

"No, I don't need to see it again. And no, I can't explain it. It's not my job to try and explain things that can't be explained—that's your job. And if you guys don't have anything further, I'm going to have to ask you to leave."

"You seem quite upset," Detective Porter said.

"Well, you barge into my home and start accusing me of killing a woman and having an affair in front of my wife, so yeah, I'm a little upset."

"Maybe there's a logical explanation for all of this, Mr. Harstow. That's why we came over. We want to clear your name and move on to finding out who the killer is," Porter said.

"And I'd like to point out that neither of us accused you of killing this woman or having an affair with her. We simply asked if you knew her," Jones added.

"Well, like I said, I don't know the woman, and I can't help you. And I think I'd like to have my lawyer present before I answer any further questions. If I'm not under arrest, I'm asking you to leave my home."

Porter spoke up again. "This woman was robbed and shot twice at point-blank range. She deserves justice, don't you think?"

Before John could respond, the front door burst open and Max came in.

"Mom, why are there—"

"I'm not sure, dear, but I think they were just leaving," I said, looking over at the men.

"Yeah, I believe so. If we have any more questions, we'll be in touch," Jones said as he and Porter headed for the front door.

Jones reached the door and turned around. "Stay in town, Mr. Harstow. We may end up having a few more questions for you."

John remained seated with his hands cupping his lips. I could tell he was more than a little pissed.

"Mom, tell me what's going on. Who the hell were those guys?"

"You watch your mouth, young man," John said.

Max glared at him but said nothing. Then he whirled around and ran back out the door. Ten seconds later, I heard his car crank up. The tires squealed as he peeled out of the driveway.

I closed the door and walked over to John.

"Did you do it?" I asked him.

John whipped his head around and glared at me. "Did I do what?"

"Lexi. Did you kill her? And if you did, why?"

John said nothing. Instead he sat motionless paralyzed by my question.

"I know about Lexi, John. No more lies."

In that moment, the wall of deceit and deception crumbled around us. John stared at me and said nothing.

Chapter 19

"So, did you kill her?"

"No."

"Did you love her?"

He didn't answer, and I decided that I wasn't going to speak again until he did. I wasn't bailing him out of this one.

"It's hard to explain, Candy."

"No, John, it's not. Did you love her?"

"Well, as we both just found out, she's dead now, so what's it matter?"

I wanted more answers, but right now it seemed we had more pressing issues—namely, whether or not John had a hand in killing Lexi.

"So if you didn't kill her, why were there cops here asking you about it?"

"I don't know, Candice. Trust me, I wish I did."

I pushed him in the chest. "John, damn it, what do you know? Do you know anything? You don't know if you loved her. You don't know why the cops were here. Jesus!"

Finally all of my anger and hurt had boiled over. "Talk, John. From start to finish. I want to know it all."

Oftentimes, when we humans say "I want to know it all," we really don't mean it. Yeah, we've all said the words before. The anticipation feels good. This was one of those times when I wanted to know it all, though the details would probably just bring me more pain and heartache.

"I'll start at the beginning. I met Lexi—"

I shook my head. "Stop. Maybe in a few days I'll want those details. For now, just tell me why they think you're involved with her murder."

John took a deep breath. "Lexi was a spy. And she was running guns for the Russians."

I sat in disbelief. "A spy?"

If he'd told me that after I met Lexi the first time, I would have laughed. But after meeting her the second time, I believed it.

He grimaced. "Yes. I didn't know it when we first met, but I found out shortly thereafter."

"So you were having an affair with a Russian spy. This is unbelievable. And Jeremy?"

"What about him?"

"The things he was accusing you of . . . ?"

"He was right."

"So were you stealing American secrets and passing them on to your piece of ass? How could you be so stupid? Did you ever once stop to think about what it could do to me? To Max? To us? Obviously not. The only thing on your mind was getting laid."

Saying Max's name must have struck a chord deep inside John. He broke down, crying and begging for forgiveness. No matter the situation, watching a grown man cry always did something to me.

I didn't hug John or offer any words of consolation. I just waited. When he finally calmed some, I asked my next question. "So you think these people killed Lexi? The Russians that she worked for? Why would they want her dead?"

He nodded.

"Can you prove it? Seems like they've got you pegged as their bad guy."

"Maybe. But these guys are professionals, so maybe not."

"Is there a chance that they'll come after you next? Are we safe, John, me and Max?"

He said nothing.

"I guess you hadn't gotten this far in the thought process when you starting banging her."

He buried his head in his hands. I knew I could shoot barbs all day, but in the end that wouldn't help us out any.

"I'm sorry," I said.

"No, don't apologize for anything. I deserve any and all of the mean, hateful things you want to say to me. I don't know if I could have messed this up any worse."

"John, you are one of the smartest men I know. Think. We need a move here. What are you going to do? What are we going to do?"

Chapter 20

The sun's rays blasted through the curtains and settled on my face. I rolled toward John and watched the peaceful rise and fall of his chest as he slept.

It had been two days since Detectives Jones and Porter stopped by. John stayed out late both nights. He wouldn't tell me what he was hatching—"plausible deniability," he said—but I knew it was big. What I didn't know was if the plan, whatever it was, would work.

I'd noticed black Tahoes moving in and out of the neighborhood. I couldn't tell if they were cops or Russian hit men.

The doorbell rang, and I rolled toward the window to check the clock radio on the dresser. It was eight twenty-five. Who in the hell is ringing my doorbell this early on a Saturday morning? I wondered.

I threw on my robe to go downstairs. John hadn't moved, so I shook him. "John, wake up. Someone just rang the doorbell."

Normally, someone ringing the doorbell wouldn't signify any type of emergency, but right now we couldn't be too careful. He slid into his slippers and led the way downstairs.

John opened the door, and there stood Detectives Jones and Porter and a street cop.

"Detectives, to what do I owe the surprise?"

"Mr. Harstow, we are going to need you to come down to the station and answer a few questions," Jones said.

"Why can't I answer them right here?" he said, eyeing the three of them.

The uniformed officer juggled the set of cuffs he was holding.

"We need to get a few things put into this case file—officially," Jones added.

"Am I under arrest?"

"Not yet," Porter jabbed.

John eyed him. I leaned into John's ear. "Let's just go."

We got dressed, called our lawyer to meet us downtown, and headed out.

We found a parking spot right in front of the station.

"I'm sorry about all of this, Candice," John said as he turned off the ignition.

I nodded. "I know. C'mon."

They put John in an interrogation room where our lawyer waited. The room I was led to was adjacent to John's. I could see him through the window and could hear what they were saying, but he couldn't see me.

Jones and Porter entered the interrogation room and closed the door behind them.

"Mr. Harstow, my name is Detective Jones. I am the lead detective assigned to Lexi Price's murder. Please understand that this entire session is being recorded, both audio and video. Can you state your name for the record?"

"John Michael Harstow," he said, his voice barely more than a whisper.

"Can you speak up, Mr. Harstow?"

John repeated his name and glared at Jones.

"Can you explain to us the nature of your relationship with the deceased, Ms. Price?"

John looked over at Tom, our lawyer, who nodded.

"We were friends."

Jones laughed.

"Something funny?" John asked.

"Friends, Mr. Harstow?"

"Friends. You do have friends, don't you, Mr. Jones? Or does the missus not let you have friends?"

"I'm not going to play games with you, asshole. I know you—"

Porter grabbed Jones' arm.

"Listen, detective. I'm a very busy and successful businessman. I have a full schedule, even on the weekends. I'd like to hurry this up, if we could. You asked about our relationship and I answered. Next?"

"Were you romantically involved with Ms. Price?"

Again John looked over at Tom who, this time, shook his head.

"Next question. Being friends doesn't imply romance in the least. You make of it what you want."

"Moving on, where were you on the night on July tenth?"

"I'd have to take a look at my calendar and get back to you. Like I said, I'm a busy man, and that was several weeks ago. To be fair to both of us, I'd need to check my calendar."

"Fair enough. Next question. You ever heard of an operation called Klondike?"

"Can't say that I have."

"I want to get back to Lexi Price—your friend. Me and Detective Porter here stopped by a few days ago, and I showed you a picture. Do you recall?"

"Yes. What about it?"

"Well, I'm having a problem here. You see, you just told me that Lexi was your friend, but when I showed you the picture of her, you claimed you didn't know the woman."

"The picture you showed me was of the bloody remains of someone who had been shot in the face. So no, I didn't recognize her in that photograph."

"Boy, you are one sharp cookie, aren't you?" Jones said. "You know what? I'm done here—for now."

"So I'm free to go?"

"That's what I said. And you better hurry before I change my mind," Jones said, flipping off the recording devices.

John stood up. "That a threat, detective?"

"Listen, mister. I always get the last laugh. You'd be wise to remember that. Like I said, get the hell out of here before I change my mind."

Tom ushered John toward the door before he could respond.

"You'll be back here soon enough, don't worry," Jones added, a final parting shot.

"Let it go, John," Tom said. "It's not worth the fight. You know that."

They left the interrogation room, and I met them in the hallway.

"Candice, can you get this sharp cookie home?" Tom said, laughing.

Despite everything that was happening, even John cracked a grin at that one.

We headed for the car and made the drive home in silence. There was simply nothing more to say.

Chapter 21

John looked down at his watch again. Prodinov's men were supposed to be here by now. His instructions had been clear: 0900 @ Houston ship channel. He took out his binoculars and zeroed in on the area where he'd told the men he would be. Panning left one hundred yards and back to the right, he still saw no one.

By killing Lexi, Prodinov had sent a message loud and clear to all of his men—and to John—about double-crossing him. Now it was John's turn to send a message back equally as loud.

But where the hell were they? Had he been stood up?

Just then he got a message on his burner phone.

Where are you?

I'm here.

We don't see you.

Nor do I see you.

We are walking down now.

You will see me when I see you – that was the agreement.

No problem, American friend.

Three minutes later, John saw the caravan of Russians. Prodinov's men had told John to come alone, which meant there was no way that he would actually do it. He'd called in some favors from retired military friends who also sat hidden among the docks.

After the caravan stopped, four men climbed out of one of the vehicles. John waited another minute, but that appeared to be it.

We are here, still we do not see you.

I see the four of you. Headed your way.

John climbed down from his hiding spot. He stopped, took out his silencer, and screwed it onto his weapon.

He took his second burner phone out and texted his team.

Heading down, intercept in five.

When he finally approached Prodinov's men, two of them quickly headed his way.

Instinctively, he pulled out his weapon and pointed it at them. Both men responded by doing the same.

"Everyone calm," Ricco belted out. "Let us not act in haste, friends."

"Why does he have a weapon?" one of the men asked.

"I have a weapon for the same reasons that you do," John replied. "You asked me to come alone, and you expected me not to have a weapon?"

Ricco walked toward his men and whispered something John couldn't hear. Slowly, the men lowered their weapons.

"Now, friend, can you put your weapon away?" Ricco asked.

John tucked his nine back into the waistband of his pants.

"So we are here. What news do you have for Alexander?" Ricco asked.

John reached into his pocket and took out an envelope. "I have a letter for you to give him."

"Why can't you just tell me, friend?"

"This way he can read the letter over and over again."

John walked over and handed Ricco the letter. "The envelope is sealed and for his eyes only. That going to be a problem?"

Ricco smiled. "No problem here, boss."

"Good," John said.

"You really think whatever this letter says is going to save your life?"

John smiled. "No, not entirely. But it's only a small part of my message."

"Oh yeah?" Ricco asked, cocking his head.

"Yeah. Let me ask you a question now."

"Shoot, Cowboy."

"You guys know everything about me, right? Or at least you think you do."

"Cowboy, we know everything about you. Hell, we know everything about your goddamn parents," Ricco said, sharing a laugh with his crew.

John laughed too. "Well, I thought so, but when I contacted you for tonight's meeting, you accepted."

"And? Listen to this guy, will ya?" Ricco said, pointing at John.

"If you knew me as well as you say you do . . . well, frankly, you would never have shown up here."

Ricco took three steps and stopped just inches away from John's face.

"And what the hell does that mean, Cowboy? You gonna take out that little gun and shoot us all one by one while the rest of us sit back and watch?"

"See? There you go again, Ricco. You guys don't know me if you think I would try something so idiotic."

"Well, you were stupid enough to have an affair with a Russian spy, weren't you?"

John wagged his finger. "You got me there, Ricco. But you see, that was just a lack of judgement, not a barometer of my intelligence. As it turns out, it was a very poor choice, it seems. I mean, look at me now, right?"

Before Ricco could get another word in, John's squadron of retired military hit men, all trained killers, had them surrounded.

"What? What is this, man?" a startled Ricco asked.

Two guns were pointed at Ricco from either side. The rest of his crew had Glock barrels pressed against their foreheads.

John took a step toward Ricco. "Like I said, if you really knew me, you never would have showed up here. I was trained to kill lazy, no-good dipshits like you. I've hunted and trapped men way smarter than you."

Ricco put his hands up. "Okay, you made your point. Now, you let us go, and I won't even tell Alexander about this."

John smirked. "Listen to you. You sound pathetic. Growing up, my father told me, 'Son, if you ever point a gun at a man, you'd better shoot it.'"

"Listen, we'll give you anything you want. Just name your price."

John yanked his gun out of his waistband. He rushed Ricco and smashed the barrel into his skull. "No, asshole, you can't bring back what I want. One of you put a bullet in the head of what I wanted. Was it you?"

"No. No way, man. Listen, we are sorry about Nika, but you got it all wrong."

John waved his gun at the other men. "You think this man gives a shit about you?" he said to them.

Then he turned back to Ricco. "It's time for you to sing, little bird. Which one of them shot her?"

Ricco said nothing. John chambered a round. "Last time I'll ask, little bird. Which one of you assholes shot Lexi? That's the one I'm going to kill first."

"We didn't kill her man, I swear."

"You lying piece of shit. You'll say anything to save your life, won't you?"

Ricco shook his head. "I'm telling—"

The words barely left Ricco's mouth before the first round went off. One of Prodinov's men reached for his gun, and the battle began. Within seconds, three of the four Russian goons were down before they'd even had time to unholster their weapons. Only Ricco remained standing.

"Harstow, listen to me," Ricco whined.

John snapped his wrist, connecting with Ricco's throat. The man went down hard to his knees.

"Shut up. Don't say another word," John hissed. "You're only alive for one reason. You take this letter to Prodinov and tell him to find another kid to bully. Make it crystal-clear too, Ricco. Me and my family are off-limits. Otherwise, both you and Prodinov will end up just like the three of these bozos. Nod if you understand."

Ricco nodded, and just as quickly as they'd swooped in, John and his soldier friends were gone.

Chapter 22

I was lying in bed reading Lee Child's new book when I heard the door opening downstairs. It was a few minutes before midnight. This was another one of those times when I wanted to know everything but wanted to know nothing too.

John had quite a mess on his hands. He had a lot of military buddies, even several HPD pals like Jeremy, so at least I could take comfort in knowing that whatever it was he was into, he wouldn't be going it alone.

I didn't go downstairs to greet John. Not this time. I'd let him have his time to decompress from the night's work, whatever it had been. He'd come upstairs when he was ready.

Fifteen minutes later our bedroom door eased open.

"Hey," I said.

"Hey," he called back.

I smiled. "Don't mind me saying this, but you look like shit."

He laughed. "Rough night, but for what it's worth, I think half of our battle is over. Please don't—"

I waved him off. "No need to worry. No questions from me. Why don't you hop in the shower and then come to bed. You've got to be drained. You've been going like this for days now."

"I'll follow that order. But you know I've done fifty-hour recon missions with no sleep. This is child's play."

"This is also at forty-plus and not twenty one years old," I said with a chuckle.

"Very keen observation."

"You'll feel it tomorrow," I added.

John took off his shirt, and even at nearly fifty his muscles still bulged. He stripped down to his boxers, and then those came off too.

"Something I can help you with, young lady?"

"No, sir, there's not," I said, burying my head in my book again.

"Uh-uh. Okay."

He headed for the shower, leaving me alone in our bedroom. Five minutes later, the bathroom door flew open, and what happened next caught even me by surprise. John, still soaking wet, marched over to the bed, bent down, and scooped me up into his arms.

"What are you doing, John?"

"What am I doing? I'm about to make love to my wife."

"And what about my clothes, John?" I said, laughing.

"They're just clothes. Besides, they've been wet before."

He carried me into the shower and pushed me back against the wall. It didn't take long before my nightgown was completely soaked. John cupped my face with his hands and kissed me. I swear the kiss lasted longer than any kiss in our twenty-year relationship.

With his lips still pressed to mine, John peeled off my gown and flung it over the shower wall.

He put his hands on my hips and turned me around. I stretched out my arms to brace myself on the wall and arched my back, inviting John to enter me. This time I wouldn't stop him. This time I wouldn't say no. I needed this. He needed this. And we lost ourselves over and over again.

The next morning when I awoke, I found myself using John for a pillow. I reached my hand under the comforter and trailed my fingers along John's inner thigh. If he wanted to go another round, I wasn't going to say no this time either. I couldn't even remember the last time we'd had sex two days in a row. Probably sometime during our early twenties, which was pretty pathetic.

"You trying to start something you won't be able to finish, young lady?" he said.

"What? Bring it on, mister. You don't scare me."

And then, just like a few days earlier, the doorbell rang. John and I stared at each other.

Without a word from either of us, we slipped out of bed and went down to open the door. John looked through the peephole and then back at me.

"It's those damn detectives again. Jones and Porter," John said, opening the door. "Well, isn't this getting to be fun?"

"Not my idea of fun," Jones muttered.

"Or mine," Porter added.

"You here to arrest me? If not, I'm closing the door."

"May we come in?" Jones asked.

John rolled his eyes and stepped aside, ushering them in with a sweep of his hand. "By all means, be my guest."

Jones and Porter took up their places on the love seat again.

"Can I offer either of you gentlemen something to drink? Coffee? Tea?" I asked.

"No, ma'am, we're fine," Jones said.

"I don't think we'll be here very long, ma'am," Porter offered up.

"So what seems to be the problem this time, boys?" John said.

"Well, we found out your Lexi friend was really a girl named Nika. You aware of that, Mr. Harstow?" Porter asked.

"I don't recall hearing that, no."

"You love playing those word games, don't you?" Jones said.

"If by word game you mean 'I don't recall,' well then you've got me dead to rights."

"Your friend, as it turns out, was running guns and drugs for a powerful Russian organization. We couldn't find a name for the group, but our initial research shows that they're well organized," Porter added.

"Guns? Drugs?" John tried to act surprise. I don't think he fooled anyone, but it was worth a shot.

The two detectives looked at each other. "Yes, both, Mr. Harstow. We also are starting to believe these guys are the ones responsible for her murder. That isn't confirmed, but it's looking that way. One of the holes we have right now is motive. You know why these guys might have wanted your friend dead?" Porter asked.

John shook his head.

"Hmm. You ever heard of Alexander Prodinov, Mr. Harstow?"

Again John shook his head.

"Well, we find it extremely odd that your friend was murdered and then, a few nights later, the men we think killed her wind up dead. Don't you find that odd, John?" Jones asked.

"I'm uncertain as to what you're trying to say here."

"Where were you last night, Mr. Harstow?" Porter asked.

"Home. I was here."

"All night? Can anyone corroborate that?" Porter asked.

"Yes. All night. Well, I take that back. I took Max to the airport. He's attending a football camp at a university he's interested in."

"So can we talk to him?" Porter asked.

"He'll be back in a few days. You can talk to him then."

"We'll do that. Is it possible that you could have forgotten about the drive to the ship channel to get some payback on Prodinov for killing your . . . friend? Or maybe you're just not able to recall?" Jones asked.

John laughed.

"Glad you think this is amusing. When the big boys have you grabbing those ankles, you won't find it so funny," Jones said. "And we've done some research on this guy. Not sure he's someone you want to piss off," he added.

"You do realize you went from one murder rap to at least three?" Porter said.

"I realize that every time someone winds up dead, you come knocking on my door. No proof, no evidence, no witnesses. I don't know . . . seems like harassment to me. Maybe even abuse of power."

"Oh there's evidence," Jones said, smirking.

"There can't be any evidence linking me to a crime I didn't commit. Unless it's planted or something you guys have drummed up. Cops have been known to do that when they really want to stick it to someone."

Chapter 23

Twenty minutes later, they were still grilling John, hoping for anything that conflicted with what he'd already told them.

The muffled buzzing of a cell phone caught the men off guard, but they ignored it until it stopped. A few seconds later, it began again. All three men pulled their phones from their pockets. Only John's was vibrating.

"Must be a wrong number," he said as he rejected the call.

"Do you know who it could be?" Porter said, pointing to the phone.

John shook his head. "No. I don't recognize the number."

"But I didn't ask you if you recognized the number. I asked if you knew who it could be," Porter countered.

John shrugged and shook his head again. As he tucked his phone back in his pocket, my phone started buzzing. I hit the ignore button and showed John the screen. It was a strange international number. Who the hell could it be?

Five seconds later, Detective Porter's phone buzzed in his hand. He stared down at it, gave Jones a worried look, and answered it.

"Detective Porter. Who am I speaking to?"

"Hello?" the man said in a thick, raspy, Russian accent.

"Uhh . . . hello. Can I help you, mister . . .?"

Porter put the phone on speaker and muted the line for a second.

"How the hell did he get our phone numbers? And how did he know we were all here right now?" Porter asked.

Jones crawled over to the window and peered out. He shook his head to indicate he'd seen nothing.

"Mr. Prodinov. And yes, you can help me. Could you start by giving the phone to John, please?"

We all stared blankly at each other.

"I'm afraid not. Listen, we're kind of busy right now. Maybe John will give you a shout-out after we leave," Porter added.

"No, Mr. Porter, this cannot wait any longer. You see, I have a pressing issue with John."

"Listen, it can and will wait."

"Porter, you seem like a nice guy. But arguing with me is a quick way to make a lifetime enemy, and that isn't something you want."

Jones reached out and muted the phone again.

"Porter, let's play nice and see what he gives us," Jones said. Porter agreed and unmuted the phone.

"Okay, so here's the deal. We will turn the phone over to John, but the speakerphone will be turned on," Porter said. "Oh, and how about you not threaten me again?"

"I'm not in the business of making deals. And your voice hurts my ears, Mr. Porter," Prodinov added. "And I don't make threats that I can't carry out."

"You've got some nerve. I usually take a little longer to decide that I don't like a guy," Porter said.

"I need to teach you a lesson in manners. I asked you nicely, and yet you still refuse. Remember that we had this talk," Prodinov said. "And as for you, Mr. Harstow . . . would you care to explain how three of my men died last night at your hand, and why?"

Jones and Porter stared hard at John now.

"Why does everyone think I'm just going around murdering people?" John asked no one in particular.

"You will pay with your life, Mr. Harstow, and the lives of your family!" Prodinov growled.

The call ended and for a minute no one said a word.

"Well now, it seems like we aren't the only ones curious about your whereabouts last night," Jones said.

"Here in America, evidence gets convictions. Not little hairs on the back of your neck or some crazy theory you or someone else might think makes sense," John said.

"We'll get the evidence. Don't worry about that," Porter added.

Both detectives stood up. "Like we told you a few days back, don't leave town," Jones said.

I walked over and opened the door to let them out. Everything inside of me wanted to ask John what'd happened, but I knew better.

"I'm scared, John," I said, watching from the window as the detectives pulled out of the driveway and sped away.

"Come here. Nothing is going to happen to you or Max. You're going to be fine. I promise."

I stared up at him but said nothing.

"I know right now my promises don't mean very much," John said.

"I signed up for richer or poorer, better or worse," I said.

John smiled. "Well, I think we can agree this is definitely not the better end of the deal."

I couldn't even manage a smile.

Chapter 24

It should be clear now why the day that I found the condoms in John's pocket had been the second-worst day of my life. And the burning question—what could possibly be worse?—continued to be answered, day after day after miserable day. That one day had set off a series of events that could easily be described as hell. Sometimes when we're in the middle of a bad situation there's a "Jolly Jody" in our lives who spouts out something like, "It could always be worse." Well, this time she was right.

After we received the call from Prodinov, we were all on high alert. A few of John's old military friends were patrolling the house, rotating on twenty-four-hour shifts.

The past few days I'd caught myself peeking out the window every five to ten minutes. Not like it was going to help, but I really didn't know what else to do.

"Candice?" I heard John call me from the staircase.

I turned around. "Yes?"

"Max's plane lands in twenty minutes. We should get a move on."

I hated involving Max, but the detectives wanted to see if his story matched what John had told them. At this point, with so much time gone by, it seemed a little silly to me. We'd obviously had days to tell Max exactly what we wanted him to say. John told me that they probably weren't concerned about that, because their advanced interrogation techniques could sniff out that type of thing.

After we arrived at the airport, I waited in the car while John went inside to meet Max. Thirty minutes later, the two of them finally appeared.

"Hey, Mom," Max said as he slid into the back seat.

"Hey, Max. How was the trip? Did you like the campus?"

"I loved it. I believe I'll be calling SMU home next football season."

"You sure have made your mom and me proud, Max," John said as we merged into highway traffic. "I'll be the first one to say I don't like getting you involved with this . . . other stuff, but we have to get it over with."

Max stared out the window and said nothing. I wondered if their relationship would ever heal.

"Max, this shouldn't take long, okay?" I said as John parked the car in front of the police station. "The detectives should only have a few questions for you."

"It's okay, Mom. Let's just get it over with. I'm ready to be home."

"I know you are, dear."

We'd called ahead, and even though it was after eight p.m., both Jones and Porter were waiting for us.

The three of us were escorted back to one of the interrogation rooms. This time, because they were interviewing Max, who was still a minor, both John and I were allowed to stay in the room with him.

We waited, alone, for at least ten minutes.

"Mom, what's taking so long?" Max finally asked.

"They know we're here. They're just playing mind games with you, son. Trying to make you nervous. It's okay. You'll do fine," John said.

Another five minutes went by before the door finally opened.

"Mr. and Mrs. Harstow, so good to see you. And you must be Max," Jones said.

"Yes, sir. Nice to meet you."

"Big, good looking kid. How tall are you, son? Six three, six four?"

"Actually, I'm six five," Max answered.

"Wow! Impressive," Porter said before introducing himself. "And your dad's what, six two maybe? Not many six-foot-five guys running around," he added.

"So Mr. and Mrs. Harstow, we wanted to bring Max in and ask him a few questions about the other night. And maybe he can fill us in on his dad's behavior the past few months," Jones said.

"You told me you wanted to ask him to corroborate my story," John said.

"Well, we did say that, but this is an ongoing investigation, and over the past three days . . . well, we've continued to investigate. I mean, that is what we do. Just a few more questions we came up with is all," Jones said.

"You okay with that, Max?" Porter asked him.

Max shrugged. This must have been one of their techniques—along with freezing us out. It couldn't have been more than sixty degrees in there. All in an effort to make the three of us uncomfortable.

"I'll be asking all the questions from here on out, Max, to make it easy for you," Jones said.

Max said nothing.

"So tell me, in your own words, the last few months . . . how have they been for you?"

"Fine, I guess. I'm not sure what you mean, really."

"I mean just in general—school, home, socially."

"School's been okay, and my social life is great."

Jones looked up from his clipboard and stared at Max. "And home?"

Max glanced at John and me. "Home's been a challenge at times."

"Care to talk about it?"

John interrupted. "What is this, a therapy session or an investigation?"

"Mr. Harstow, I'd hate to have to ask you to leave the room. We're trying to do our jobs. Please." He turned his attention back to Max. "I'm sorry, Max. You were about to tell us about your home life?" Jones said.

"Well, it's been tough at times. We don't really talk about it much—or at all, really."

"I'm sorry, Max. I don't want to make any assumptions here. When you say 'we don't talk about it much,' what exactly is the 'it' you're referring to?"

Max cracked his knuckles and fidgeted in his seat but said nothing.

"We're all friends here, Max. You can say whatever it is you need to," Jones said.

Max stared at John. "The 'it' was my dad never being home. Mom and I are there for each other, so it's okay."

A single tear rolled down John's face.

"Well, I'm sorry to hear that, Max. I'm certain that couldn't have made you or your mom too happy."

Jones pulled three pictures from a file folder and slid them across the table.

"We told you some new evidence had been uncovered during the last three days, Mr. Harstow. These are pictures of the man who we believe killed Lexi Price."

John leaned up to the table and took one of the pictures in his hand. I moved closer to the table to get a look at them too.

"Why do I need to see these?" John asked. "None of them are me. I told you guys I didn't do it."

"Well, Mr. Harstow, the pictures are a little too grainy to make out facial features."

Jones took out two more pictures and slid them across the table.

"Okay, and what are we looking at here?" John asked.

"Same man. The photos came from a bank ATM about a mile away from Lexi Price's murder scene."

"So?" John slid the photos back to Jones.

"Whoever did this was smart, Mr. Harstow. It was dark out, so the pictures don't really help much with identification. And the assailant wore dark-colored clothes to help blend in even more. But there are a few things that he can't change," Porter said.

"You want to tell us again where you were that night, Mr. Harstow?"

"Not really. I've already given an official statement you can refer to. My answers haven't changed," John said.

"What about you, Max?"

Max looked dumbfounded by the question. "What about me?"

"The night of July second. Can you tell us where you were?"

"Max was at study hall that night, so he couldn't tell you where John was . . . if that's your next question," I quickly interrupted.

Jones picked up one of the pictures. "We had a forensic scientist look over the pictures. He couldn't make a positive ID, because it was simply too dark. But what he could nail down was height and build. Using the surrounding objects as reference points, he deducted that our guy was . . . what, Detective Porter?"

Porter rifled through some papers on the table in front of him. "Let's see . . . approximately six four or six five," he said.

Suddenly, the air in the room got heavy. I grabbed my chest, because it felt like the next breath wasn't coming. A shot of adrenaline jolted through my veins. What the hell was this man saying? I looked over at Max. His eyes instantly filled with a rage that I had never seen before.

"Mrs. Harstow, are you okay?" Jones asked.

"I'll be fine. Max? Baby?"

Max turned to John. "She deserved it. If I would have found out who she was sooner I—"

John slammed his hand on the table. "What are you talking about, Max? Stop this foolish talk right now! Don't you say another word."

"No, Dad. It's too late now. It's over—football, school, my future. You have to live with this! I'm glad your little tramp girlfriend is dead!"

"No, Max!" I yelled.

"Yes, Mom. Every night I watched you sit all alone. I saw the pain in your eyes, the hurt. I wanted to make him pay for hurting you. I wanted to make her pay too, and I did!"

"Max, son, these guys will use everything you say against you. Stop please. Give yourself a chance."

Max stood and towered over John. "A chance? Give myself a chance? I had a godammned chance. I had two loving parents and a good home. I was athletic enough to play big-time college football. And I had a hypocritical dad who couldn't keep his dick in his pants."

"Are you saying that you killed Lexi Price, Max?" Jones asked.

My body heaved as tears poured from my eyes. Max was seventeen, which meant they'd try him as an adult. And here in Texas we had the death penalty, which would probably be on the table. My marriage—hell, my life—was effectively over. What was left, other than watching Max go to trial and plead guilty to murder, divorcing John, and watching Max turn old on death row until finally they gave him the needle? In an instant, everything I'd built and dreamed of was gone.

If you couldn't get up each day with something to look forward to, why would you keep getting up?

Think, Candice.

I jumped across the table, and before Jones could react, I knocked his service weapon onto the ground. I dove on top of it, put the gun to my head, and pulled the—

Chapter 25

John Harstow watched as they lowered his wife's coffin into the ground. He could see Candice's dad, Gus, and her sister as they consoled each other. John was, by his estimate, two hundred and fifty yards away from the service, which he hoped was far enough to avoid being seen. Gus had never fancied John, and now, after everything that'd happened, he didn't want to add to their grief by showing up.

Max hadn't been granted leave to attend his mother's funeral. And he hadn't accepted any of John's visits to see him. The prosecution was throwing the book at Max, charging him with premeditated first-degree murder and seeking the death penalty. John had used all of their savings and hired the best defense lawyer in the state of Texas, Olivia Donavan, but so far Max had declined all of her visits as well. John pulled a few favors and had Max on suicide watch.

After the service John headed back to his house—their house. Back to nothing and no one. Everything and everyone he'd loved—Candice, Max, even Lexi—was gone.

He opened the door and threw his keys onto the table by the front door. He wandered into the kitchen and opened Candice's wine cabinet. He turned several bottles around to read the labels. He was looking for the oldest and most expensive bottle he could find.

Finally he found what he was looking for, a 1941 bottle of Inglenook Cabernet Sauvignon that'd been given to Candice as a gift. The bottle had been worth over twenty thousand dollars a few years earlier. And he wanted to know what a twenty-thousand-dollar bottle of wine tasted like.

He found the opener and popped the cork on the expensive bottle. One of Candice's wine glasses sat a few feet in front of him on the counter. He grabbed it and poured a full glass. After he set the bottle down, he swirled the wine around in the glass.

As he sat down at the bar, he felt the cold barrel of a gun on the back of his head.

"You always knew Mr. Prodinov was going to win, right?"

John nodded. "It's easy to win though, when you're the only one playing the game."

"You tried the wine yet?"

John shook his head. "Not yet. I figured I had a little more time."

"Funeral's over, right?"

John nodded.

"I'll make you a deal, Harstow. If you don't try any funny business, I'll let you finish the glass."

John held the glass in the air. "I'll take you up on that offer. Pour yourself a glass, if you'd like. It's not every day you get to pop open a bottle of wine worth twenty thousand dollars."

"Thanks, but no thanks," the man said.

John never turned around. He didn't need to see the killer's face.

He took a sip of the wine. "Didn't think there'd be much of a difference, but I must say it's good." He turned the glass up, finishing the rest of the wine in one gulp.

He stared up at a family picture that hung in the living room. A tear rolled down his cheek.

"You ready?" the man asked.

He nodded. "Can you do me a favor?" John said, reaching into his shirt pocket. "Can you drop this in the mail for me? I was going to take it on my way to the funeral, but I forgot. It's for my son, Max. Last seven words he'll hear from me."

"Sure. But why seven words?"

"The number seven is used all throughout the Bible. Seven is a holy number, they say. But this just so happened to be seven words. It wasn't a plan or anything. Really, it's all I got left. Hell, maybe it is a holy number after all."

"Makes sense in a weird way, I guess. Time's a-tickin'. Let's do this, Harstow."

John took a deep breath and closed his eyes.

The big man pressed the barrel of the gun to the back of John's head and squeezed. Harstow was gone now, and curiosity got the best of the killer. He tore open the envelope that Harstow had given him:

You didn't deserve this – I love you.

The man set the letter on the bar and left.

THE END

***

***

About the Author

Terry Keys is an award winning novelist, songwriter, and poet. Keys spent time working in law enforcement and corrections; he now writes for Examiner.com and works in the oil and gas industry. A native of Rosharon, Texas, Keys spends his free time hunting, fishing, and working out. He lives in Dickinson, Texas, with his wife and two children.

Read More from Terry Keys

www.terrykeysbooks.com

Made in the USA
Middletown, DE
03 December 2019